BEH●LDER
Crowned

BOOK FOUR OF THE BEHOLDER SERIES
CHRISTINA BAUER

Monster
House
Books

First Published by Monster House Books, LLC in 2017
Monster House Books, LLC
34 Chandler Place Newton, MA 02464
www.monsterhousebooks.com

ISBN 9781945723223

For the Special Education Teachers at the Countryside School
in Newton, MA.
Because they work real magick every day.

CHAPTER ONE

It was never a good idea to spy on the gods, as a rule.

That said, I was never one to follow the rules.

All of which was why I now stood in a hilltop ringed with skulls, staring out over a deserted landscape. A shiver of foreboding rolled across my shoulders. This place gave new meaning to the word *bleak*. Ashen soil stretched off in every direction. Charcoal-colored clouds wheeled overhead. A freestanding archway made from chipped stone loomed nearby. The thing looked like a ruin, but it was actually a magickal gateway called the Skullock Passage. Soon, this archway would also serve as my supernatural keyhole for spying on the gods. Quite possibly, I'd be killed in the process.

Considering my situation, it was a risk worth taking.

I glanced up at the darkening sky.

Almost time to begin.

Any minute now, a slash of blood-red light would appear by the horizon, marking the arrival of the Martyr's Comet, a heavenly body that showed itself once every two thousand years.

Unfortunately, the Martyr's Comet had all sorts of dark legends surrounding it, such as the prophecy that whoever was the strongest Necromancer alive when the comet appeared, then that same Necromancer had to die when the comet vanished.

This particular legend had changed my life from bad to worse.

First, the bad part. About two months ago, my one-time Mother Superior, Petra, informed me of the Martyr's Comet prophecy, including the bit about the strongest Necromancer dying. That was certainly bad news; some poor mage was supposedly doomed.

Second, the worse part. Then Petra shared that I was the strongest Necromancer alive and she planned to end my life when the comet vanished. In other words, about three days from now. As I said, worse.

Of course, I'd no intention of dying any time soon. I just needed more information so I could foil Petra's schemes—hence my spying expedition.

A flicker of light appeared at the horizon. My gaze locked on the spot. Was that the Martyr's Comet?

I squinted into the darkening sky. The brightness clearly shone white, not red.

Only a shooting star, then.

A weight of disappointment settled on my shoulders. In some ways, I was looking forward to the comet's arrival. With it, there came additional powers over gateways, especially for mages like me. Tapping into those extra abilities, I'd turn the Skullock Passage into my personal spy-hole.

Take that, Petra.

A small cloud of dust began spinning on the ground nearby. The particles whirled in curlicue shapes that were too perfect to be natural. *Magick.* My heart lightened. Perhaps my mate Rowan was arriving. I had expected him to magickally transport here any second.

Sadly enough, blue lights sparkled deep within the haze. A weight of dread settled into my bones. Someone was casting a transport spell, only it wasn't Rowan. My mate was a Creation Caster, so his power came from life and his magick glowed red.

This brightness shone blue, which meant the visiting mage was a Necromancer like me.

Damn.

Most likely, Petra was sending yet another messenger my way, asking me to fulfill the Prophecy of the Martyr's Comet and die willingly on the comet's last day. Meeting these messengers was never pleasant, but it wasn't particularly dangerous, either. Petra wouldn't try to kill me until the Martyr's Comet was just about to disappear.

Small comfort, really.

Within seconds, a wisp of a girl materialized beside me. She looked about sixteen years old with large brown eyes, pale skin, and raven-dark hair. The image of her skull had been magickally marked onto her face in dark tones. Her clothes were long black robes decorated with a few ties, which was the formal dress for a Sister, the lowest level of initiated Necromancer.

The girl spied me, gasped, and fell to her knees. A small puff of dried earth flew up where she landed. "Greetings, my Tsarina."

I pinched the bridge of my nose. All Petra's messengers fell on their knees when they first laid eyes on me. It was rather unsettling. I wasn't this girl's Tsarina, and even if I were, bowing and scraping weren't my idea of fun.

"I'm Elea. Just Elea. What's your name?"

The girl clasped her hands under her chin. "I am called Petra's Echo."

Not again. Petra was forever renaming her followers. So far this week, I'd met Petra's Consolation, Petra's Light, Petra's Patience, and now, Petra's Echo. It was demeaning to steal away someone's identity in such a manner. My one-time Mother Superior was turning crueler by the day.

"What's your *real* name?" I asked.

"I gave it to you. Being called Petra's Echo is an honor for me."

It was an effort not to roll my eyes. Should I fight her on this point? *Perhaps.* This girl seemed more open and innocent than my past messengers, so I might be able to break past Petra's brainwashing. Plus, I did have some time before both Rowan and the comet arrived. I decided to test the waters. "How about I call you Echo?"

"Whatever you wish, Tsarina."

I fought the urge to smile. None of the other messengers had allowed me to de-Petra their names. Maybe I could help this girl.

Echo glanced nervously around, as if Petra might be lurking under a nearby rock. "But make no mistake. Everything that I am today comes from Petra and Petra alone. I owe her my life."

I sniffed. "That's not how I remember it happening. As I recall, there was a great battle. On one side, there was the evil mage Viktor. On the other side, there was me and my mate Rowan. During the fighting, I summoned an army of Necromancers back from the dead to help win the day. You have my skull-mark on your face. That means you were one of those mages. Petra played no part in it."

"Oh, how disrespectful I have been to you, my Tsarina." Echo leaned deeper into her kneel, stopping only when her forehead slammed against the ground. "You did indeed raise my physical body from the dead. However, Petra has since renewed my soul. I beg you to forgive me. Hear my vow: I promise to worship you as well, my Tsarina."

"That's not what I meant." I knelt beside her. "I wish you wouldn't worship Petra or me. When you regained your mortal body, it's true that my death magick reached out to your spirit. But never forget—it was *your* will that tapped into my spell. You hauled yourself back into the realm of the living. On its own, my skills couldn't have done that. Power and light dance inside you; those are yours alone. Don't ever give credit for them to someone else. Not even me."

Echo angled her head against the dusty earth, stopping when her gaze met mine. "This is all a trick." Her voice quavered. "You are testing my faith."

"No, I'm trying to help you. How about we both stand up?"

"As you command." Echo hopped upright and stared wide-eyed toward the horizon. When she spoke again, her voice held the singsong notes of a trained speech. "My name is Petra's Echo. You are our Tsarina, born Elea of Braddock Farm. You raised my body from the dead, and now my soul is led by Petra, the Most Holy Messenger of the Gods."

"The list of Petra's titles grows by the day." With slow movements, I forced myself to rise once more. "You'd best share what you came to tell me." I glanced up at the sky. No red slash of light; the Martyr's Comet had yet to arrive. There was still time to convince this girl.

Echo kept speaking in her singsong tone. "Petra is the Mouthpiece of the Gods, and she has a request for you. Our people believe you are our Tsarina."

"I'm aware." When I refused to take over ruling the Necromancers, Petra simply told everyone I was leading them from afar. It was most annoying.

"The Mouthpiece of the Gods has trusted me with a great secret." Echo lowered her voice to a whisper. "You are not truly our Tsarina. You haven't completed the sacred rites."

I sighed. "I'm aware of that as well."

"Don't you want to be Tsarina? You'll be hailed as the strongest Necromancer alive."

"That's precisely why I don't want the title. Right now, being confirmed as the strongest Necromancer isn't exactly a good thing." I shook my head. "Not that you'd know that. The messengers never receive all the necessary information."

"That doesn't make any sense. The Divine Petra has told me everything I need to know. Her message to you is this: complete the rituals and take over your true mantle as our Tsarina. Cease your pointless refusals."

Here we go again. Every missive from Petra was the same, as was my response, which always came in the form of a question. "And has Petra told you *why* I refuse?"

"Not specifically."

Because she never does. I'm sure Petra wouldn't find so many willing messengers if they knew the truth. No one wants to tell someone powerful that they must die soon. "Did Petra give you totem rings, by any chance?"

"Two of them. It is an honor." Echo lifted her dainty hands. She wore two silver thumb bands carved in skull patterns—the classic sign of Petra's totem ring creations. The reason for the bands was simple. Necromancer spells required exceedingly long incantations. Grand Mistresses could load magick onto rings and activate them with a single word.

"She always sends one messenger and two totem rings." I shook my head. "Those bands aren't a gift; they're a means of controlling you. Petra has loaded that first ring with a memory wipe spell. It will activate once we're done talking, usually when you speak the formal Necromancer farewell, *valedictions*. The second band is loaded with a transport spell to bring you back to Petra's side. That one will launch when you say the word *transport*."

"You're wrong about the totem rings, you know." Echo lifted her right hand. "This isn't a transport spell."

I narrowed my eyes. "What is it then?"

"A secret."

"I see." This girl was proving tough to reach. It was time to call in my best weapon. "You never answered my question. Do you wish to know the truth about why I refuse to become Tsarina?"

Echo hugged her elbows for a moment. Then, she nodded.

"Good." I gestured to the rickety arch behind me. "This is a gateway. Have you seen any before?"

"Yes, there's one hidden in our Cloister. It leads to another world—the Eternal Lands of the Sire and Lady."

"Quite right. The Sire of Souls and the Lady of Creation fashioned all the magickal arches in our world. Most of them lead to the Eternal Lands, but some connect elsewhere instead. In fact, legend tells of a place called the Meadow of Many Gateways where the arches link to nothing but other worlds." I gestured to the night sky. "Every two thousand years, the Martyr's Comet appears and weakens these gateways. Since our world has been magickally tied to so many others, we can't risk those arches falling apart. The very foundations of this world would collapse."

Echo popped her hand over her mouth. "Is that true?"

"Unfortunately." As if to highlight the point, a low rumble shook the earth. These quakes were becoming more and more common. "Up until this point, Petra and I believe the same things. But what I'm about to tell you next? That is where we differ. Petra also believes that the Martyr's Comet carries with it a prophecy. Have you heard of it?"

Echo frowned. "A prophecy related to the Martyr's Comet? Never."

"I hadn't heard of it either until a few months ago. This prophecy states that when the Martyr's Comet arrives, the greatest mage must sacrifice their life and power into one of these very gateways. The arch will then soak in their magick, distribute it to the other gateways, and maintain our world. The most powerful Necromancer alive is supposed to rule our kind. As a result every two thousand years, our Tsar or Tsarina always sacrifices themselves to the gateways."

Echo blinked. "I don't understand. You need to die?"

"The Martyr's Comet will appear any minute now. It will then cross by the horizon and vanish in three day's time. At the end of the third day, Petra plans to kill me and toss my body onto one of these gateways. But I won't let it happen."

This last part was a bit of a lie. I'd cast vision spells, pored over ancient texts, consulted Seers, and hired legions of mortal researchers. All of them confirmed that some unlucky Necromancer always died to fulfill the prophecy of the Martyr's Comet. According to every vision spell and Seer, the next sacrifice would never be Viktor, a homicidal mage who was my preferred choice for the job. No, all the scholars and visionaries agreed: the sacrifice was likely to be me.

I could see the logic, sadly enough. Viktor was also locked off in exile. Even if he could be set free, I'd need the Sword and perfect timing in order to have him be the sacrifice. It was far better for all of us if I had a back-up plan.

Echo's pretty features fell slack with chock. "Everything will fall apart without the gateways having magick. You said so yourself. Don't you want to save our world?"

"I do, but there's always more than one way to accomplish any task. In my case, I am mated to Rowan, a Creation Caster. We've shared our Necromancer and Caster energies to create a new kind of hybrid magick. It's incredibly powerful. In fact, I think it could fix these gateways. But Rowan and I need access to the gateways in order to test out our spells." We also needed to spy on the gods for more information before the testing could begin, but I didn't volunteer that fact.

"Oh, that won't happen. The Sire and Lady have warded every gateway. You can't even approach them safely, let alone cast a spell."

"I've noticed." I scanned the dark sky again. "Once the comet appears, that will change. I'll be able to cast a spell or two."

"And the Sire and Lady will allow that?"

"No, unfortunately. I've pleaded with them for information about the gateways and hybrid magick. They've refused. They won't even lower the wards so I can test out a few minor spells. Don't you think that's suspicious? Shouldn't I be allowed to try something else before giving up my life?"

Echo stared at her totem things. "This is all very confusing. I'm failing at my task."

Poor Echo. She seemed so deflated and miserable. "Look, you've failed at nothing. Petra has no real verbal message for me today. She merely sends Sisters like you to show me that she can get to me whenever she wants to…And she plans to find me at on the third day of the Martyr's Comet."

Echo twisted her totem rings in a nervous rhythm. "The Mouthpiece of the Gods warned me that you wouldn't agree. But I'm not to transport back to her like the others. I'm to activate this totem ring, bringing the Divine Petra here to speak to you directly."

I frowned. This was different for Petra, and with the Martyr's Comet about to appear, I didn't like things changing, especially with someone as young and inexperienced as Echo around.

"Listen to me carefully, Echo. Do not speak the word to launch that ring."

Echo went on anyway. "Possession!" With that word, Echo's totem ring flared with blue light. Instantly, an indigo haze enveloped the girl. Her eyes took on a glazed and empty look. When she spoke again, Echo's voice had a distinct monotone. "I have taken control of this lesser mage. Now I give my true message to you, Elea."

I'd heard that voice many times before. *Petra.* She'd cast a spell of possession on young Echo. A chill of fear crawled up my limbs. This wouldn't end well.

I cupped my hand by my mouth. "If you can hear me, Echo, you need to stop speaking."

On reflex, I reached out with my mage senses, getting ready to cast a counter-spell. Necromancer power lay all around me, resting heavily in the bones and fossil-laden rocks under the earth's surface. I drew that energy into my soul. Magick flowed into my limbs, making the bones in my arms glow blue with power.

When Echo spoke again, it was still with Petra's voice. "You'll never pull in enough power in time to help this lesser mage. You must stop fighting me and pay attention. You have forced me to possess this girl's body because I must teach you a lesson. When you disobey the gods, *this* what happens to those you love."

Blue light flared once more from Echo's totem ring. More possession spells. With unnatural speed, Echo turned to face the deadly gateway.

I gasped. "No!"

Without so much as a glance in my direction, Echo rushed toward the magickal arch at a supernatural pace. I quickly glanced upward. The Martyr's Comet still hadn't appeared. Echo was headed toward a gateway that remained fully warded and absolutely deadly. I simply had to stop her.

I raced toward the girl. "Wait!"

But Echo didn't seem to hear my words. Just as Petra had predicted, there wasn't time for me to cast a spell or catch up by running, especially considering Echo's magickal burst of speed.

I could only watch in horror as the young girl stepped under the arch. For a moment, Echo stood frozen in place. After that, her body took on a glass-like sheen, like she was made of porcelain instead of flesh and blood. Blue light illuminated her from within. Dark fissures formed along her skin and robes. My heart cracked as well.

The gateway's magick was about to pull Echo apart.

With a great boom, Echo shattered into a thousand glowing shards of blue light that flew into the illuminated stones of the gateway. For a moment, the arch's rocks flared with such a bright shade of blue, they almost looked white. A weight of sadness settled into my soul. There was no coming back when you were obliterated by a gateway.

Echo was dead.

Around me, everything reverted to its non-magickal state. The gateway's stones returned to being non-illuminated blocks of gray. I stared down at my arms. Blue light still shone in my bones. *There's still so much power in my body, all of it ready to cast a counter-spell.* Plus, if Rowan had been here, we could have brought hybrid magick into the mix as well. *That was even more energy.*

And yet, I couldn't save that innocent girl.

Echo was gone, but her words—or I should say, Petra's— reverberated through my soul: *"When you disobey the gods, this is what happens to those you love."*

Petra kills them.

Meaning I should sacrifice myself or she'd take those I cared about.

Waves of rage tightened up my rib cage. Petra had moved on from sending threatening messengers to murdering mages before my eyes. My one-time Mother Superior had made her point: she would do anything to force my sacrifice, one way or another. And there was no question who she planned to go after next.

Those I love.

Rowan.

If Petra's intention was to frighten me into submission, it didn't work. With each passing moment, more of my will hardened into stony resolve. *I would still spy on the gods and get some answers.* Then I'd use that information to learn hybrid magick and fix the gateways.

And after all that, I'd make Petra pay for what she'd done to Echo.

CHAPTER TWO

I wasn't sure how long I stood staring at the darkened stones of the gateway. The image of Echo's unlined face kept appearing in my mind's eye. I was about her age when I first went to Petra for training.

Petra.

I'd never known my own parents; they'd died soon after I was born. Over my years of learning at the Cloister, Petra had become more than my Mother Superior. She was the closest thing I had to a living parent.

And now, she was murdering innocents so I'd take over ruling the Necromancers and fulfill the prophecy of the Martyr's Comet.

What a catastrophe.

A small cloud of red dust spun on the nearby earth. Waves of ethereal warmth rolled up my limbs. I knew this magickal signature. My mate Rowan was transporting to join me. *At last.*

Rowan and I were true Caster mates, which meant we shared our magick. As a Necromancer, my power came from the remnants of life around me, such as bones and dried leaves. Meanwhile, Rowan was a senior Creation Caster. His magick was drawn from living things. During castings, my energy shone with blue light; Rowan's glowed crimson. When we were in each other's presence, we could mix our magick together into hybrid power. In those cases, our energy shone violet.

The nearby swirling mists changed. Crimson lights began dancing inside the haze. My heart soared. This was definitely a Caster spell. Seconds later, Rowan himself materialized beside me. He stood tall with his broad build, muscular limbs, and strong bone structure. Today he wore battle leathers and a concerned look in his green eyes. He immediately wrapped his heavy arms around me. "What's wrong?"

I leaned into his touch and sympathy. How wonderful to have someone know me so well that, without saying a word, it was clear that I was struggling. I quickly explained what had happened with Echo and Petra. As I spoke, Rowan rubbed my back in soothing circles.

When I finished my tale, Rowan kissed the top of my head. "Shall I tell you a story?"

I pressed my cheek against his chest and grinned. Rowan was forever telling me Caster tales. One of my favorites concerned a raven. "Please do."

"Once upon a time, there was a powerful king."

"Was he handsome?"

"We'll get to that part." Rowan chuckled, and his rumbling laugh reverberated through my entire body. Already, I was feeling better.

"I can't wait," I said.

"This king was supposed to meet his lovely mate for a some-what dangerous enterprise involving isolated gateways and spying on the gods."

"The mate in your story sounds rather marvelous."

"Exceedingly so." Although I couldn't see his face, I could easily picture the happy look that now danced in Rowan's green eyes. "Back to my story. This king was due to use his magick and trans-port himself to his wonderful mate when some gray-haired ladies knocked on the main gates to the castle."

"How fearsome." I mock-shivered.

"Just you wait. These wise ladies informed the king that the community had decided to hold an elder festival."

I rolled my eyes. "You Casters and your parties."

All of Rowan's people loved to celebrate. And since Rowan was the Caster king—what they called their Genesis Rex—he always made a point to fully enjoy the fun.

"Normally, that is the case," said Rowan. "But elder festivals are a little different sort of celebration. The great king had to make toasts in the honor of more than a hundred elderly ladies."

I leaned back and looked up into Rowan's face. "And why do I get the feeling that you—I mean, that the king in this story— didn't enjoy that?"

A sneaky gleam shone in Rowan's eyes; that meant he was getting to the good part of his tale. "Elder toasts involve a senior lady asking the king to raise a mug in their honor. The toast is then followed by a chaste kiss on the cheek. Or, at least it's supposed to be chaste." Rowan lowered his voice to a conspiratorial tone. "Some of the ladies got carried away."

I couldn't help but smile. Rowan always knew how to break my sad moods. "So that's the moral of your story: you were late tonight because there was too much royal smooching to be done?"

"And some of my subjects have rather bad breath."

Now, I outright laughed. "When I become Caster queen, will I be asked to perform the same service for the elder Caster men?"

Rowan gave me an overly serious look. "I'm afraid so."

"In that case, I refuse to take the crown." An edge crept into my voice that I hadn't meant to put there. "You can't force me. Don't even try."

Rowan cupped my face in his hands. "Never. No one would ever strong-arm you into take the Caster crown, not like..." His unspoken words hung in the air.

Not like Petra, forcing me to become Tsarina.

Thinking of Petra shattered my good mood. There were questions to be answered, and the Martyr's Comet would only last for three days. I stepped away from Rowan's hold and scanned the skies. A crimson streak now glowed by the horizon. "The Martyr's Comet is here." Saying that aloud made my spying mission suddenly seem a waste of time. "The wards are now lowered on the arches. Maybe we should just experiment with hybrid magick. See if we can heal the gateways on our own."

"We asked the Seers about that. Cast a dozen vision spells. You know what they all said."

"I do." For some reason, the Sire and Lady were reluctant to hurt or imprison me. However, that would all change if I used hybrid magick directly onto the gateways. We'd be imprisoned or dead in a heartbeat. It seemed strange but then, who understood the mind of the gods?

"Your plan is a solid one, Elea. Our best hope is to cast a spying spell and see what we can discover. After that, well…You know we have one more option."

"Tossing Viktor's body into the gateway?"

Rowan grinned. "You know that is my first choice."

"Mine as well." Sadly, none of the Seers or experts thought that would come to pass. There were simply too many variables: freeing Viktor and then getting him to the right spot at the correct moment. Oh, and then there was the matter of my conscience; I wouldn't murder someone unless they attacked. No, hybrid magick was a far better route. Which brought us back to finding information.

And indeed, Rowan had another option on that score.

The Martyr's Comet not only lessened the wards on gateways, it also made it easier for mages to travel between them. There was one world in particular that held some alternative deities who might help.

The world of the trickster gods. I shivered. That was one place I'd no desire to visit.

"In that case, let's hope our spying mission works." I squared my shoulders and lifted my chin. "I'm ready to begin."

"I have every faith in you." Rowan kissed my forehead. "You *will* do this, Elea."

My mate seemed to believe my façade of fearlessness, but inside? I kept picturing what had happened to Echo—how her body was torn apart by the wards protecting this very gateway.

It was never a good idea to spy on the gods as a rule.

Perhaps this would be the time my law-breaking tendencies caught up with me.

CHAPTER THREE

Rowan rubbed his palms up my arms. His touch was firm and grounding. "What spell will you cast?"

My gaze locked on the ruined gateway. Over the past few weeks, I'd spent hours in ancient archives and royal libraries, researching different magickal approaches to spying through gateways. Based on my research, it was clear that using hybrid magick on the gateway was out of the question—the gods might sense the unusual power signature, and any hope of stealth would be lost. I might as well set off a firecracker in their faces. In the end, there was only one spell I could choose.

I gave Rowan's hand a squeeze. "I plan to cast a Moon Dial. It will show me all conversations that might interest us. I'll see anything that happened through the last full moon."

Rowan dropped my hand. "But that's a high level spell. You'll be deeply weakened. Why not cast something that shows the past? We want to find out how they made the gateways, after all."

"With those spells, I won't be guaranteed to see anything. I may only have one chance at this; I simply must get some information.

And over the past weeks, I've made dozens of requests for access to the gateways so we could test out our hybrid magick. The Sire and Lady must have discussed something about my queries, especially since they've refused them all."

Rowan stared at the gateway with such intensity I thought his irises might light up with power. "Agreed. Moon Dial it is. And I'll stay nearby, ready to cast a spell in case anything goes wrong."

His words made a weight of worry ease from my spine. Knowing Rowan would be nearby was a great comfort. "Thank you."

"Only, I want to be ready with more than Caster magick."

I knew what he meant. If everything went south, it wouldn't matter what kind of magick we used, so long as it was strong. Rowan needed to be ready with hybrid power.

Rowan held up his hands with his palms toward me. "Charge me up?"

"With pleasure."

Lifting my hands, I rested my palms against Rowan's. This motion was different than merely touching or holding hands. For me and Rowan to create hybrid magick, we needed to touch skin-to-skin with the intent to share power. Only then would we create a mixture of Necromancer and Caster energy.

Rowan leaned forward until our foreheads met. This wasn't necessary for us to share magick. It felt wonderful, though. Touching Rowan was its own kind of magick; the moment we were in contact, I instantly felt better.

Closing my eyes, I pulled Necromancer power into my body. Within seconds, I found caches of gazelle bones under the ground. These were rich with memory and magick. I drew the energy into my body, a power so strong I could almost feel the lithe animals racing across a faraway landscape. Necromancer energy thrummed through my limbs, so I focused the power into my forearms. The bones there glowed blue. My skin turned chilly to the touch.

At the same time, Rowan was pulling Caster power into himself as well. Soon his hands warmed with magick from living things. His energy arced from his hands into my fingertips, tickling my palms.

Opening my eyes, I found Rowan watching me intently. Every line of his face seemed to brim over with adoration. A blush colored my cheeks. "What have I done to deserve that particular stare?"

"And what look is that?"

"The one that says I hung the sun and moon."

My mate gave me one of his crooked smiles. "You didn't?"

Rowan moved in closer until his lips brushed against mine. "Let's share magick." With that, my mate opened up the circuit between us. Blood-red light brightened his hand. Small arcs flared between our palms as the crimson flow of his magick poured through my left palm. Once inside my soul, Rowan's boiling-hot Caster power mixed with my chilly Necromancer magick. Swirls of chill and heat tumbled around my chest before flowing up through my right arm. As the power moved down my right hand and back into Rowan's palm, the color of the energy changed.

Violet in hue.

Hybrid in power.

The energy moved between us until every corner of my soul felt filled with the warmth of our joined magick.

After that, it was time to let that hybrid magick settle into Rowan's soul. For our plan to work, the hybrid energy needed to be in him, not me. If I carried any, the echo would stay in my magick, and that might set off the wards.

I lowered my left hand so Rowan could no longer feed fresh Caster energy into my body. My right hand was still connected to his left, though. Through that link, I continued to pour the hybrid energy I'd built up into my mate's soul. Purple veins of light brightened across Rowan's arms and chest as the power built up inside him. The sense of warmth and fulfillment emptied from my body. Once I'd given up all my hybrid energy, I pulled my right hand away as well.

The link between me and Rowan was severed. For a moment, the purple light in Rowan's skin flared more brightly, then it slowly faded. The power hadn't disappeared from my mate, though. The energy was only being held in reserve until Rowan needed it…

Which hopefully wouldn't come to pass. But when it came to spying on the gods, you never knew what would happen.

I rested my palm against Rowan's cheek. "Is that enough power?"

Rowan leaned in to my touch. "More than enough. You should recharge before casting."

"True." Closing my eyes, I pulled in fresh Necromancer magick from the environment. Once my soul felt full again, I focused the energy into my arm until my bones there glowed blue. I focused on Rowan. "I'm ready."

Rowan stepped back and winked. "I love to see you cast."

Another blush colored my cheeks. Perhaps one day I would be so accustomed to Rowan's compliments, his words would never cause my face to burn red. I wasn't anywhere near that day yet, however.

"Remember, once the spell starts, we won't be able to speak."

"Not with words." Rowan gave me another crooked smile. We were able to say many things to each other with merely a look. The thought gave me more confidence. Rowan and I shared more than magick. We were a team. I knew that together, we could do this.

I turned my attention toward the lopsided blocks that made up one of the most powerful gateways in existence.

Time to cast my spell. Keeping the power focused in my arms, I spoke the first part of my incantation.

Search from birth to death
Awakening to dream
Illuminate what I seek
Wield magick and moonbeam

I raised my arms above my head. Beams of magickal energy arced between my palms, making me think of blue lightning. I tamed the power and focused it toward the empty area underneath the gateway.

Then I set my magick loose.

Long jagged lines of energy shot toward the gateway. The blue bolts ricocheted under the arch, creating what looked like a blue spider web of energy. I finished my spell.

Eternity and moments
Horizon and sky
Search the moon's cycle
Give me vision to scry

More bolts of power appeared under the gateway until they merged into a single sheet of blue light, a brilliance that filled the once-empty place under the stone arch. A circle of white appeared in the center of that blue panel. It was this white shape—looking like a full moon—that gave the spell its name. Excitement sped through my bloodstream.

This was it. The incantation worked!

I focused on Rowan. He stood unmoving only a yard away. Light crackled and pulsed under the archway, sending uneven bursts of blue light over his stoic form. For a moment, he looked more like a statue than a person.

My strong mate.

Rowan voice cut through the growing darkness. "You can do this, Elea."

I refocused on the gateway. This will work. My legs felt wobbly as I stepped up to the arch. Reaching forward, I gripped the glowing white circle and turned it to the left, activating the spell.

Images appeared under the gateway. There was the Sire of Souls, seated on a tall dark throne in his castle of shadows. His black armor reflected the shifting light from nearby torches.

I glanced over my shoulder at Rowan. His gaze was locked on me. I gestured to the gateway. Speaking would be easier, but it could also set off the wards. My question was present but unspoken. Can you see this?

Rowan shook his head. No.

Turning around, I refocused on the vision that only I could see.

The Sire stayed seated on his throne. Not speaking. Not helping, either. I reached forward. As my hand neared the space under the gateway, the Moon Dial appeared again. I turned the circular shape once more.

Images under the gateway changed. Next I saw the Lady of Creation as she strolled through her garden. She was a vision of loveliness with her sun-browned skin, sky-blue gown, and tiny golden slippers. As the Lady sauntered by, flowers bloomed around her. Trees erupted in fresh green leaves, their branches seeming to reach toward her. While the Sire had been hidden in shadows, the Lady stayed bathed in buttercup-yellow sunlight that reflected off her long sheet of golden hair, which trailed behind her.

This was a beautiful sight, but not particularly useful. Surely, they had to speak to each other about the gateways and hybrid magick! I spun the Moon Dial again. The scene under the gateway changed once more.

Please, let this be something helpful.

Now, the Lady walked up the long set of stairs that led to the Sire's throne. Unlike the other scenes, I could both see and hear the action. My breath caught. This could indeed be what I was looking for. The Lady paused before the Sire, cupped his face in her hands, and gifted him with a deep kiss.

I winced. This was a personal moment between husband and wife. It seemed wrong to intrude. However, I couldn't deny the spark of hope that had lit up in my chest.

This was really working.

"The Martyr's Comet will appear in seven days," said the Lady. Her voice was like sunshine and bells ringing.

Seven days. That meant this spell was showing me a vision of the recent past.

For a few seconds, the Sire merely stared at her intently without saying a word. The man was all things beautiful and pale with his dark hair and haunted grey eyes. While the Lady vibrated with energy, he seemed to be still as stone. "Viktor will test his army again tonight."

The Lady frowned. The expression made my heart crack with grief. I had the urge to rush into the gateway's image and force her to smile again. "Do not worry, my love," she said brightly. "Viktor's power over hybrid magick is limited."

"You've said that before. I'm not so certain he isn't a threat."

"Oh, we've handled his sort before." The Lady grinned again, and it felt like the clouds parting after a storm.

"But we've never handled one like Elea and this Caster of hers. Their hybrid power is too strong."

"They have no idea what it can do. We have nothing to fear."

The Sire raised his hand. It was a small movement, but coming from the Sire, it seemed dramatic. "Hybrid magick always fails." The pale skin of his hand flared with violet light.

Hybrid energy.

The gods wielded hybrid power? I suppose it made sense. The Sire was the ultimate Necromancer. The Lady wielded Caster energy. The two of them were clearly mates. Why wouldn't they have hybrid magick?

The Lady frowned once more. "Don't access that power. It's dangerous."

Even so, the Sire kept his hand glowing purple with the hybrid energy. I marveled at the beauty of the violet light beaming from his skin. This was a far more intense brightness than what Rowan and I could conjure.

"We used hybrid magick to build the gateways and unite the worlds. With this power, we created our empire." The skin on his hand darkened, the flesh bubbling like tar. "Who knew the energy would turn on us?"

"Stop, my love."

The black tar look crawled up his arm, bubbling as it went. "We united these worlds, and they call us tyrants. Conquerors." The tar look bubbled up his neck. "The hybrid power is ours, and yet we can no longer wield it."

"But we found the Vortex Realm, didn't we? What a silly little land it is, what with its minor Casters and Necromancers. We taught them true magick and then united all the connecting arches into the Meadow of Many Gateways. And hybrid magick? It's no longer necessary. We figured out how to tap into the power of the Martyr's Comet so we could recharge the gateways without wielding hybrid magick. There is nothing to fret over. Our rule is safe."

The Sire lowered his arm and released the magick. Little by little, his skin returned to its normal pale hue. "But this girl. This Elea. She wants to use hybrid power on the gateways."

"She'll die if she tries. Even I don't remember how we first created the arches so many millennia ago. Trust me, this Elea will see the error of her ways. She'll soon accept that death comes for all mortals. The only choice they have is whether to make sure that their loss counts for something. What a great gift we've given her—the chance to renew the Meadow of Many Gateways, protect her world, and solidify our rule."

On reflex, I set my hand on my throat. My dying for their gateways was a great gift? Did she really say that? And to solidify their rule when their subjects called them tyrants? I knew the gateways connected the realms, but I didn't realize the Sire and Lady ruled them. I only knew that they oversaw ours.

I turned to Rowan and opened my mouth, ready to tell him everything.

Rowan lifted his hand, palm forward. I knew that gesture. Wait. His eyes narrowed. I knew my mate well enough to know what expression meant as well. Is everything all right?

I waved my hand dismissively. I am fine. I wanted to tell Rowan about what I'd learned right now, but that speaking might activate the wards.

The Lady rested her hand on her husband's dark skin. "This Elea doesn't want our realms, my love. She'll answer the call. She's a good girl, like all the ones before her."

The Sire's voice turned deep as thunder. "And if she isn't good?"

The image in the gateway began to fade in and out of focus. A hum of energy filled the air.

The spell was starting to unravel.

I could only hear parts of what the Sire next said. "Sword of Theodora…army…her friend Amelia."

A band of fear tightened around my throat. Amelia was a kind soul and my best and only friend. What would the gods want with her? Was she already in danger?

The spell broke further. Bands of blue light frayed even more. The image of the Sire and Lady became nothing but a blur. On reflex, I cursed my luck. "Damn."

That word was all it took. The gateway wards swung into action. The bans of blue light snapped free from the image and reached out to me, wrapping about my wrists and ankles. The chill of Necromancer magick bit into my skin.

Rowan moved to stand before me. "Elea," he whispered. "What's wrong?"

The blue cords of power wound more tightly around my ankles and wrists. "Can you see these?"

Rowan summoned hybrid power until the skin of his right hand glowed with power. He spoke one quick phrase. "Grant me sight." After that, Rowan wiped his fingertips across his eyes. His irises flared with purple light. "I see them now. The wards are going after you. I don't like it but…"

I knew that tone to my mate's voice. "But what?"

"The wards are acting as a buffer between us and the gods. They can no longer tell if we're using hybrid magick. We could try a few tests, if you like."

"Not yet. The gods talked about Amelia; I have to discover what they meant. Help me turn the dial once more." The fact that we were now speaking to each other caused the wards to pull me further, but there was no stopping it now.

Rowan gripped my wrist, pulling my arm free from the blue cords. I reached forward and turned the Moon Dial once more.

The image under the gateway changed again, and what I saw stole my breath away. Under the arch was a vision: one of the villages where Changed Ones lived. These were Creation Casters who'd been transformed by Viktor's experiments. Every so often, one of them would lose their minds, attacking anyone around them. As a result, the Changed Ones had decided to relocate and live separately. Lately, a few of those settlements had disappeared. We'd figured they must have simply moved to new ground. A chill crawled up my neck.

"I'm seeing a new vision under the gateway," I told Rowan. "Those missing Changed Ones. I fear something awful may have happened to them."

I'd gotten too slack about the gateway's wards. Speaking was a sure way to trip over more layers to these complex ward spells. Now those protections struck out with a vengeance.

Fresh cords whipped out from the gateway, gripping me about the knees and elbows. My teeth chattered from the ethereal cold. I knew what this ward spell was. Frozen Death. I couldn't move. I couldn't cast. And if this casting wasn't broken soon, my heart would freeze, and that would end my life.

"I pulling you out of this spell," warned Rowan.

Panic was vibrating through my bones, but I was a trained Necromancer. When I spoke again, I was the image of calm. "One more minute, please."

In the image under the gateway, a Changed One stepped into view. It was a teenage boy with a heart-shaped face. Caster mages developed familiars or animals that they poured their soul magick into. Viktor had conducted evil experiments where he spliced the Caster mage with their familiar. As the boy stepped closer, he came into better view under the gateway. His legs had been replaced with those of a lion.

How horrible.

Suddenly, a burst of violet light encircled the boy, and he transformed from a human with the legs of a lion to a full hybrid lion-man. These Changed Ones could no longer cast spells, which meant this magick came from someone else: Viktor. I couldn't believe what I saw. What had once been a boy was now mostly a lion. The only difference was that the new creature stood on its hind legs.

This wasn't just hybrid magick.

Viktor had created hybrid people as well. Did the Sire and Lady know about this? Was this all part of the army that they'd mentioned before? The Sire and Lady said that Viktor was testing out his warriors. It would make sense that these Changed Ones were actually some kind of proto-form before they took their final shape. Beside the man-lion appeared a hybrid of a cheetah. Another was a praying mantis.

With that, these one-time Casters began tearing one another apart.

My heart sank. We'd gotten reports of villages of Changed Ones disappearing without a trace. Is that what happened to them? Viktor had been conducting tests to turn them into mindless killing machines?

Fresh cords of Necromancer magick wound up my limbs. My entire body convulsed.

I heard someone screaming, and I realized it was me. "Now, Rowan! Set me free!"

Rowan gripped my forearms tightly. A loud ringing echoed in my ears; it was some kind of side effect of the ward spell. I saw Rowan's mouth moving, so I knew he was speaking an incantation of his own. Somewhere in my mind, I registered that purple light was shining out from beneath the skin on his arms.

This was no ordinary spell. Rowan was speaking an incantation while summoning hybrid magick. His words couldn't break through the icy cords. More wound around my head. Soon, I could only see via a small break in the ropes around my face.

Rowan raised his fist. A half-dozen threads of violet-colored energy wound up his arms. Hybrid magick making tiny cords? I'd never seen anything like that before. Turning about, Rowan extended his arms toward the gateway, palms flat and forward. The threads sped from his hand and slammed into the stone.

Before, the gateway had been illuminated by a blue light—the effect of my Moon Dial Spell. Now, Rowan's threads of purple magick spun into the archway's stones, multiplying as they went. The blue light faded, along with the vision underneath the archway. Seconds later, I couldn't see the rocks anymore—there were only thousands of twisted threads in every shade of violet I'd ever seen. The tiny cords stayed in the shape of the gateway, blaring purple light over the landscape.

After that, the gateway burst apart.

The magickal cords around my body disappeared. I fell forward onto my knees. Rowan's arms wrapped around me, pulling me into his lap. "Are you all right?"

"Yes." I curled into the warmth of his chest, my teeth chattering. "What did you cast?"

"You mean those purple threads?"

"I'd never seen anything like it."

"I was trying to cast a Sun Sphere; it should have created an orb that burned through any spells around you. What happened was...unexpected."

"There's so much we don't know about hybrid magick."

Rowan kissed the top of my head. "What did you see?"

"We've been investigating what happened to the disappeared villages of Changed Ones. Viktor has been transforming them into a true blend of humans and animals. They become mindless killing machines and turn on each other. Viktor must be cleaning up all the evidence afterwards."

"I'll have the royal mages investigate."

"The Sire and Lady say Viktor is raising an army. We have to stop him."

"Viktor has a nasty habit of returning to our realm. To truly stop him, we must get the Sword of Theodora. It's the only thing that can kill him without affecting anyone else." Rowan didn't need to add that the anyone else in this scenario was me. Viktor had shown before that he could the two of us so we shared injuries.

"Agreed. We must find that Sword."

"And we will. What else did you witness?"

I went on to explain how the gods said Viktor was raising an army of Changed Ones, the strange words about the Sire and Lady gaining new worlds, and how the Lady said that it was possible to heal the gateways with hybrid power, but we probably couldn't manage it. I leaned in to my mate's arms. "I thought this would give me answers, but it just raises more questions."

"We're a step closer to the truth. You did well."

"I wish I'd learned something more about the Sword."

"Kade says Amelia has made some progress."

My heart lightened. This was great news. Some months back, Amelia had entered into a contract with Rowan to give my mate the Sword. Since Amelia was of the rightful heir to House of Theodora, her grandfather Justinian was supposed to give her the Sword as part of her birthright. At least, that's what Justinian said. Turned out, the old man lied. Amelia hadn't delivered yet on her promise to Rowan, but my friend was nothing if not persistent. If anyone could find where that weapon was hidden, it would be my Amelia.

Amelia.

I sucked in a shaky breath. "The Sire and Lady said Amelia's name." The image of carnage from the village of Changed Ones appeared in my mind. "Do you think she's safe?"

"Yes."

"But do you think—"

"Amelia and Kade are in their laboratory. How about we transport to their lab and see her for ourselves?"

I grinned. "Yes, I'd love that. Plus, I've been wanting to find out how Amelia's latest visit to Justinian turned out." Lately, Amelia and Kade had taken to camping out in front of Justinian's chateau, waiting for admittance and answers.

Rowan rubbed his chin. "I've been meaning to ask Kade the same thing."

I forced in a deep breath. The next thing I was about to say was as pleasant as eating mud. "After we visit Amelia and Kade, we need to explore that other option you mentioned for getting answers."

"You mean, asking the trickster gods?" Rowan's brows lifted. "I thought you weren't keen on that idea."

"I'm not. But after what I just saw with the Sire and Lady, it's more important than ever to get as much information as we can."

"How about we try more visioning spells? Perhaps we can ask the Seers for a new séance." Rowan snapped his fingers. "There's even an old library in the northwest of Nyumbani that we haven't explored yet."

A sickly feeling crept up my throat. How I hated this idea, but I knew it was the right thing to do. "Rowan, we've cast spells, approached Seers, and consulted hundreds of books. Neither of us wants to ask the tricksters for information, but we're out of options. The Martyr's Comet is in the sky. There are only three days left. And those tricksters can only be contacted during the Martyr's Comet. Am I right?"

"That's what the legends say." Rowan's mouth thinned to a worried line. "Supposedly, they rarely heed any summons, even during the Martyr's Comet. "

"Then we've nothing to worry about, do we?"

Rowan chuckled. "Do you ever shy from danger, Elea?"

"I may be terrified, but I'm no coward."

Rowan stepped closer. "We Casters have a saying. 'Bravery without fear is untested innocence.'" He ran his finger down my cheek. "You, my sweet mate, are very brave."

Yet again, my face burned with a fresh blush. "Let's transport off to check on Amelia."

"Allow me."

I'd fight Rowan on this, but he'd never allow me to cast after such a big spell. Besides, Rowan's transports had the added bonus of being painless. I'd yet to master that with my versions of the spell. Rowan closed his eyes and started to focus his Caster energy. As he began the transport spell, I thought through our latest plan.

After checking on Amelia, I was going to summon even more deities.

Mlinzi and Walinzi.

The trickster gods.

Combine them with the Martyr's Comet, and this situation had all the makings of a rather spectacular disaster.

CHAPTER FOUR

A few minutes later, Rowan and I materialized inside Amelia's laboratory. I shook my head, impressed. No one could cast a faster transport spell than Rowan.

The lab itself looked more cluttered than usual, and that was quite a feat for Amelia and Kade. Both of them couldn't cast spells, but Rowan and I had gifted them some hybrid power, enabling Kade and Amelia to share energy through their mate bond. That gift still didn't allow them to cast spells, however. That said, it did empower them to bare their souls to each other, which Kade thought an infinitely better kind of magick.

Most days, Rowan and I invested our time in magick and mage craft, while Kade and Amelia were obsessed with gears and steam. This entire lab was a labyrinth of tables that overflowed with springs, sheet metal, and tools of various kinds. More strips of copper and long bolts hung from the ceiling in an elaborate pulley system. The effect was like being encircled by a clockwork cloud. As a result, I couldn't see Amelia or Kade, but I did hear the steady clink-clank of metal which told me they were off tinkering somewhere.

I cupped my hand by my mouth. "Amelia? Kade?"

A chorus of clanging noises sounded. "Yow," cried Amelia. "My head."

Rowan and I shared a sly look. Amelia was forever forgetting she had hung so many metal items from the ceiling. It was a wonder the girl hadn't given herself a black eye yet.

"We've come to visit," called Rowan.

"Don't move, I'll find you," replied Kade.

As Rowan's brother made his way through the lab, the various bits of metal rattled and gonged. The place was huge, and thanks to the pulley system, it changed constantly. Within seconds, Kade appeared from around a tall pile of copper wiring. Like always, Kade reminded me of a smaller version of Rowan: he was tall and broad chested with green eyes and messy brown hair. His worn leathers held the insignia of the personal guard of Genesis Rex.

Kade wrapped Rowan in a deep hug. "Brother. It is good to see you."

"Good to be seen." Rowan glanced my way, which was my mate's way of encouraging Kade to greet me as well.

Kade turned toward me and gave a curt half-bow. "Elea."

Disappointment weighed heavily in my heart, but I leaned in to my Necromancer training to hide my emotions. I bowed slightly in return. "Kade."

Sadly, it was always this way between me and Kade. I knew Rowan wanted more. So did I, for that matter. Kade accepted me as his brother's mate, but he didn't relish the idea of having me in the royal family. I seemed to trail death and destruction behind me wherever I went.

In that sense, Kade wasn't wrong. I wouldn't necessarily want a family member caught up in my supernatural drama, either. Even so, a mate bond couldn't be denied. Even being physically separated from Rowan started an ache in my heart and bones. There was no going back now.

Amelia was next to appear from behind the curtain of gadgetry. She wore her hair in perfect red ringlets to her shoulders. Kade had made sure she had pink Caster leathers to wear instead of her flouncy gown, which Amelia adored. My friend still reminded me of a living porcelain doll, only this variety was far more ready for battle. Or in Amelia's case, blowing things up. There was no missing the scorch marks on Amelia's leathers. My friend had been running explosion tests again.

The moment Amelia laid eyes on me, she bounced on the balls of her feet. "Elea! You got our message." Before I could reply, my friend had crossed the space between us and pulled me into what I call her dance-hugs. This is where we embraced tightly while shifting our weight from foot to foot. It was all Amelia and completely wonderful.

I was so happy to see my friend it took me a few moments to realize that Amelia had said something about a message. "No, we didn't get any message from you. Rowan and I came because I spied on the Sire and Lady, and they mentioned your name. I wanted to be sure you're all right."

"That's so nice," said Amelia quickly. She grabbed my wrist and dragged me through the maze of metal.

Now, if most people had just been told they were a topic of conversation for the gods, then they'd have a lot of questions. Not Amelia. The fact that she said *that's so nice* meant my friend was leagues deep into a mechanical project of some kind and wanted me to see it right away. Nothing else mattered.

Kade, however, did not miss the comment at all. He followed one step behind Amelia and me. "Gods? What did they say about my mate?" His words came out as a snarl.

"Just listed her name, that's all," I called over my shoulder. "At the time, I couldn't hear much of what they were saying... just a snippet of a word here and there. Amelia's name was all I heard."

"May I have a minute of your time, brother?" asked Kade. That boded ill. The edge in Kade's voice said that the conversation would take far more than a minute. Kade had never been enthusiastic about our plan to spy on the gods. No doubt, he was worried that my actions were dragging my friend into danger.

Again, he wouldn't be entirely wrong.

Every so often, I wondered about hiding from the world. Perhaps I could retire to some small Cloister and wait until all this was over, one way or another. Then, I'd realize the truth. I couldn't protect myself and my friends, but leave the rest of the world to Viktor's not-so-tender mercies. After all, Rowan and I were the only ones who could fight him.

Amelia dragged me past a long curtain of what looked like metal hair and stopped at a small clearing on the lab floor. In the center of the space, there was the statue of a kneeling figure that had been made of bronze, wood, and stone. It wore scraps of black leather that had probably once been part of a Necromancer robe. Arms, legs, even the jawline…all the pieces of the statue had movable parts. It was a life-sized doll.

And it looked a lot like me.

As I stepped around the figure, the world took on a dream-like quality. Who would make a statue that looked somewhat like me? I knew the Casters were just starting to warm up to the idea of me as Rowan's mate. It seemed a little early for them to be carving statues. Besides, Caster statues were typically enchanted stone. This creation was definitely mechanical.

A dozen questions flew through my mind at once. Leaning in to my Necromancer training, I calmed my mind and selected the query that would give me the most information. "Tell me how you made this."

Amelia bounced on the balls of her feet once more. "Made this? No me. I found it! You know how Kade and I have been visiting my great grandfather, Justinian?"

"Yes." I glanced around, looking for Kade and Rowan. I couldn't see them, but I could hear their voices rumbling from not too far away. I'd have liked to have Kade here to tell his side of the story, but I supposed that would have to wait. It always took a little while for Rowan to explain why we had to do things for the best of the Casters, not only Kade's mate. It was an argument Kade never liked to hear.

"Well, on our last visit, we stopped waiting at the doorstep for entry to Justinian's chateau. Instead, Kade broke the door down, and we got into a battle with three mages." Amelia lowered her voice to a conspiratorial whisper. "It didn't go well for the mages. I used my new dart shooter on them." She pulled what looked like a miniature crossbow from her jacket. "Took them down like that."

"You killed them?" I knew Amelia had been getting battle training from Kade, but somehow I never thought she'd use it.

Kade stepped out into our group. Grinning from ear to ear, he pulled Amelia into his arms and spun her about in a circle. "Amelia had to kill those fiends; they were attacking without provocation or remorse. My mate is fearsome in battle."

Amelia set her hands on Kade's shoulders. Her big blue eyes sparkled with delight. "I wasn't that scary."

"Yes." Kade brushed a gentle kiss over her lips. "You were."

Rowan walked out of the maze and into our group. When he saw the statue, he froze in place. His eyes narrowed. "What's this? Who's making statues of Elea?"

Amelia broke free from Kade's embrace and started circling the statue, touching bits of bronze or stone as she went. "As I was saying, we broke into Justinian's castle and finally got to speak with the old goat."

"You did?" Bands of excitement tightened about my chest. *This might be the information we were looking for.* "Did he tell you where the Sword was?"

Amelia sniffed. "He said the Sword was hidden and would find me when the time was right." Amelia poked at a bit of worn leather on the statue. "The man really was useless, but then Kade had the idea to search the chateau, and we found this statue."

Kade turned to Rowan. "I had the palace mages transport it back here to the laboratory. They ran some Assessment Spells on it. The thing is made of bronze gears, wood, stone, and some small leather bits. It was made by Amelia's forebears."

"This certainly looks like the work of your family," I said.

"The mages also ran an Age Incantation on it. You won't believe the results." Kade gestured toward the kneeling figure. "That's two thousand years old."

I couldn't believe what I was hearing. "Two thousand years old? Are you certain?"

Amelia kept poking at the statue's shoulder. "Positive. They ran the spell about a dozen times."

Two thousand years old, so it was built around the last time someone was sacrificed during the Martyr's Comet. Plus, this statue looked like me and was an heirloom of Amelia's family. Instead of getting answers, every time I got more information, I only turned up more questions. In this case the query went something long the lines of: *What in blazes is going on here?*

"Did the mages get the figure to do anything else?" asked Rowan. "It looks like it was designed to move."

"The mages didn't." Kade beamed with pride. "Amelia did."

"It took some tinkering, but I got it to work a little," said Amelia. "This dolly-mech doesn't function like it should."

My brows lifted. "Dolly-mech?"

"It needed a better name than statue." Amelia pointed to the statue's base. "You can see that this was broken off from a larger set of dolly-mechs. I think there were three figures in the original piece. That's why I can't get it to do everything it was created to do, but I have gotten our dolly-mech here to say a few things." Amelia stood behind the figure and fiddled with some tiny buttons and levers on the back of its neck.

A small door on the back of the dolly-mech's head swung open. Amelia began fiddling with whatever was inside this machine's head. For a few long seconds, there was nothing but silence.

After that, the dolly-mech moved.

The figure lifted its head and opened its eyes. Metal creaked and groaned as its jaw moved. "I am Elea," it said.

Her words ricocheted around my head. *I am Elea? How can that be?*

"And she looks like you," gushed Amelia. "What are the chances?"

"What are the chances indeed," I said slowly. Other Necromancers like me had died every two thousand years for these damnable gateways. Had the girls all shared my name as well as my proposed fate? If so, it didn't bode well for me getting out of this alive.

"The Sword of Theodora is in two parts," continued the dolly-mech. "Do you have both?"

My brows lifted. "The Sword is in two parts? That's news."

The figure blinked over and over. "Do you...Do you..."

"Oops." Amelia bent over the figure again. "This happens sometimes." A soft clang sounded as Amelia fixed something inside the dolly-mech's head. "Ah, here we go."

The dolly-mech began speaking again. "The Martyr's Comet has come at last. It is time to heal the gateways. I am prepared to make my sacrifice...Sacrifice...Sacrifice..."

As the dolly-mech stayed stuck on the word *sacrifice*, I thought back to the many Necromancers like me who died to fulfill the Prophecy of the Martyr's Comet. I stepped against Rowan's side; he wrapped his arm around my shoulders.

"Yipes, she's never said that before." Amelia fiddled with the dolly-mech's head, and the figure froze in place. "Sorry about that. I'm sure you don't like being reminded of, you know." Amelia slammed the tiny door shut on the back of the dolly-mech's head. "That's all she's ever said. What an odd happenstance, finding her like we did."

Rowan pulled me closer against his side. "I don't believe in coincidences."

I leaned my cheek against Rowan's shoulder. "It's maddening. Instead of finding out what the big picture is, I keep getting more unrelated puzzle pieces. Are these dolly-mechs all part of some greater plan? If so, how?"

Amelia nibbled on her thumbnail. "So, does that mean you're going to do it? You'll call Mlinzi and Walinzi tonight?"

"That's the idea," I said. And as soon as the words left my lips, I wished they rang with more confidence. "We'll join the Festival of Monkeys and make our wish with everyone else."

Rowan kissed the top of my head. "Perhaps they won't even answer our call for information."

"It's possible," said Kade as he glared at me. I knew what the man was thinking. *It might be possible it was anyone other than Elea.*

Rowan raised his right arm, which was a sure sign he was beginning a spell. "Let's go back to our rooms and get ready. The festival starts soon, and we need to prepare. I'll cast the transport spell."

I wrapped my arms around his waist. "I'll always take you up on any offer to transport."

"I'll take that as a complement." The veins in Rowan's arm began to glow with crimson light as he pulled in more energy for his spell. Rowan glanced at Kade and Amelia. "We'll see you there, yes?"

Rowan's brother and my best friend barely had time to reply yes before Rowan and I were encircled in red smoke. The transport spell had begun.

Soon, it would be time to get ready for Mlinzi and Walinzi.

That said, I didn't know if anyone could truly be ready for trickster gods. The most I could do was expect the unexpected and hope it ended up with my having the Sword of Theodora and some way to avoid death in three days.

But that wasn't a comforting thought at all.

CHAPTER FIVE

Rowan transported us back to our cabana behind the palace. Of course, we had a formal room in the castle itself, but that was more for show. Rowan and I actually lived in this small round structure made of bamboo. It was simple, cozy, and perfect.

Once the red smoke disappeared, I noticed the thin line of moonlight peeping through the bamboo walls. After that, I noticed the touch of gentle kisses along my jawline. Rowan.

"I thought we were getting ready for the festival?" I asked. "There's a lot at stake here." *Including my life.*

"Caster culture is all about appreciating the moment. You never know what the next day will bring, let alone the next hour." Rowan kissed a slow path down my throat. "And we have at least an hour here." Rowan nipped at my neck, sending a jolt of desire through me. "And I want to take this moment with my mate." He pulled my body flush against his.

I pursed my lips and did some quick calculations. "When does the Monkey Festival begin?"

"It started hours ago, but the chance to summon the trickster gods is still quite some time away."

Rowan's kisses were distracting, but I wasn't sure at all about this Caster concept of enjoying the moment. *At least, not this particular moment.* Tonight's festival took place at Trickster's Haven, a village that was halfway across the continent. Although Rowan was strong with transport spells, it still might take us some time to get there. "Are you sure we shouldn't leave now?"

"Positive. We've plenty of time before midnight. That's when the summoning takes place." Lifting my hand, he gently brushed his lips across my ring finger and mating band. A flutter of excitement moved through me. It was true. Being held by Rowan was something to savor. "Perhaps we could wait just a few minutes more."

Rowan gave me his lopsided grin. "Now, you're making sense."

A series of heavy slamming noises boomed from the door. I'd know that particular knock anywhere, because it was no knock at all. In fact, it was more like a battering ram of a fist slamming into the thin wood. And that kind of noise typically came from only one category of Caster—Rowan's personal guard.

"My king, your presence is requested at the festival."

Rowan chuckled. "As I was about to say, it's only a matter of time before one of my guards shows up and drums us out of here."

The kisses were too delicious to end so quickly, so I mouthed two words to Rowan, *One hour?*

Surely, the Casters wouldn't notice sixty little minutes.

Rowan leaned in to nip my ear. "Yes, I think the Casters can wait another hour."

The pounding continued. "I heard that," bellowed the guard. "No one can wait an hour. The people grow too happy to listen to a speech."

Oh, no. That was guard-speak for the crowd getting too drunk too quickly. Unless we showed up and started to add some structure to the evening, the Casters could quickly turn from a celebrating crowd to a drunken mob. Those tended to be horrible to clean up.

Rowan rubbed his nose along mine. "They never pay attention to my speeches anyway."

"Your brother Jicho can't stay much longer," added the guard. Although he as still speaking through the door, the man's voice was rather loud. I wonder if the ability to yell through doors was a requirement for the personal guard. "He said to tell you that he's wanted to show you the mechanical boat he's been building with Amelia."

I gave Rowan a sad smile. "We can't miss Jicho showing us his machine ship."

Rowan slowly brushed his lips across mine. "Agreed. We'll leave immediately."

"Thank you, Genesis Rex," said the guard through the door. "We'll expect you to transport to the site within five minutes." Now, I understood that part of the guard's role was to keep Rowan on time and kingly, but they oftentimes seemed overzealous in my opinion.

Rowan shook his head. "You have my word that my mate and I will arrive in two minutes. I have more than enough magick to cast spells to alter our appearances and transport."

As a rule, mages tried not to use magick for daily skills that could be done without it. Overexposure to power warped the mind until all you could focus on was casting meaningless spells.

"That's all I needed to hear," said the guard. The pounding stopped. We really needed to give them less power over our schedule. That said, whenever we limited their access, the people ended up almost killing one another in drunken brawls.

Rowan held up his hand. "Shall we?"

"I'd like that."

He linked his fingers with mine so both our hands touched. "Then let's journey together."

And so, we did.

CHAPTER SIX

Before I knew it, Rowan's transport spell to Trickster's haven was complete. My mate and I now stood on a dry plain covered in hardy-looking ferns and a few spindly trees.

I gave Rowan's hands a gentle squeeze. "You're going to spoil me, transporting us both everywhere."

Rowan winked. "And I'm not even trying hard."

I kissed the tip of his chin. "Showoff."

"For you? Always."

I ran my fingers up his arms. When Rowan had rescued me from the gateway, threads of violet magick had wound up his limbs. It was a sign of hybrid magick at work. "Have you tried to create the cords again?"

I didn't need to clarify my question further; Rowan knew what I was asking about. We both loved innovations in spellwork. He shrugged. "A few times."

"So you've been obsessing about it ever since."

"Only every second."

Chuckling, I turned away from Rowan. He'd transported us to the base of a massive cliff carved with the images of a huge pair of monkeys. No doubt, those were representations of Mlinzi and Walinzi, the trickster gods this festival was designed to celebrate. These two giant deities were shown dancing with their arms raised. Caster runes were carved about their heads.

I pointed to the foreign words. "What do those say?"

"Welcome to Trickster's Haven. If Mlinzi and Walinzi decide to grace us with their presence, a gateway will appear at the base of this cliff wall. The village here cares for the cliff face until the next arrival of the Martyr's Comet."

"And what does that involve?"

"They clean the stone and leave offerings for the gods." Rowan pointed to the cliff base. "See those?" Small piled of flowers and dried fruit lined the ground by the cliff wall. "They are in honor of Mlinzi and Walinzi."

"And in a practical sense, the villagers also keep strangers away from these powerful gods that might be useful to Casters."

He chuckled. "My practical mate. Yes, that, too."

The cliff itself was a sheet of brown rock that split at the base. From this opening poured a great river. The main body of water was calm and dark, reflecting the comet's red glow. Many tributaries snaked off from the main body. Along the numerous connected riverbanks, there stood lines of clay houses that crawled off into the distance. Tall lookout towers highlighted the horizon line.

No sooner had we appeared than a group of Casters noticed us. They wore multicolored leathers and drunken looks on their faces. Some carried flutes and beat on drums. Behind them, others danced in circles or belted out songs. The din seemed to grow louder by the minute. Their voices rolled over me in a barrage of greetings.

"Huzzah!"

"Genesis Rex."

"Genesis Regina."

When this greeting came, I merely nodded and smiled. I'd long ago given up trying to correct the Casters on calling me Genesis Regina. It was true that I hadn't officially taken the crown of the Caster people, but to them, that was nothing but a technicality and, of course, a good reason for a future celebration of massive proportions.

Next, the group of Casters headed off into a clay dwelling where the singing soon became especially loud. I shook my head. *Casters and their celebrations.* A flock of children sped past us, trailing long strips of orange fabric on tall sticks. I realized they were supposed to represent monkey tails.

Rowan wrapped his arms around me, pulling my back against my chest. "How is my mate? You still feel well after your battle with the gateway?"

"I'm fully recovered, thank you."

"Such a shame we couldn't be together before the festival." Rowan's voice rumbled with desire.

A blush colored my cheeks. "There will be time later on."

Rowan leaned in and kissed the tip of my ear. "A lifetime, yes."

How I wished I could sit here all night, enjoying the touch of my mate. Unfortunately, we were for a very specific purpose. "Now, where do we find this Mlinzi and Walinzi?" *And the Sword of Theodora.*

"There will be a summoning ceremony at midnight." Rowan gestured around him. "Everyone gathers here, at the base of the cliff wall and calls to Mlinzi and Walinzi, asking for help with their heart's greatest desire. If the gods approve, the tricksters name the lucky supplicant and open the gateway."

"Midnight, eh?" I scanned the moon. "That's not too far away."

"Yes, I have just enough time to introduce you to the celebration of the year."

I tried to hide my smile. Not well, I had to admit. "Wasn't the last week's festival the celebration of the year?"

"It was. But this one takes place during the Martyr's Comet."

"So it's the greatest festival until the next one."

"Precisely. You're acclimating to Caster life quite well."

"Will you show me Jicho's mechanical boat along the way?"

"I'll try, but I'm afraid he's keeping the location a rather big secret." With a gentle touch, Rowan wrapped my hand around his forearm. "Let's see if we can't suss out the hiding spot?"

"That's a plan."

Together, Rowan and I proceeded through Trickster's Haven. To me, the place became a blur of clay buildings and smiling faces. The network of rivers divided the city into districts with small reedboats lining the banks. Much as I scanned every vessel, I had yet to see Jicho's mechanical ship. In fact, we both had yet to find Jicho himself. Yes, it was common for the boy to run off. Still Jicho was a nine-year old. Both Rowan and I would rather know where he was.

After we turned down a quiet street, one of the palace mages approached us. Rowan updated the mage about the missing villages of Changed Ones. I joined in, explaining what I'd seen in my vision with the Lady and Sire—how Viktor had prepped those poor Casters to turn into a deadly army. I just finished recounting my sad news when I spotted Jicho. The boy sat in a small alley between two rows of clay houses. He wore his red Seer robes and pushed a stick around in the dirt between his legs.

I stood on tiptoe and whispered in Rowan's ear. "I found Jicho."

Rowan cupped my cheek with his warm palm. "Go check on him, will you? We're almost done here anyway."

"Agreed." After saying my goodbyes, I rushed up to the alley's entrance.

"Jicho! Rowan and I have been looking for you!"

Usually, Jicho would respond with a grin and a gap-toothed smile. His happy face—combined with the shaved head that marked him as a Seer—somehow always made him seem younger than his nine years.

But there was no smile to greet me this time. Jicho merely looked up at me, shrugged, and went back to pushing a stick through the dry soil.

I glanced over to Rowan. He was still deep in conversation about what spells they could cast to find the lost Changed Ones.

It didn't seem necessary to pull him away. I stepped into the deserted passage and sat down beside the boy. "What's wrong, Jicho?"

"Nothing."

"Is that true? Normally, you're far happier to see me."

Jicho kept staring at the ground. "Sometimes, I wish I weren't a Seer."

"Have you had a vision? Something bad?"

"Yes." Jicho's voice cracked. "Worst one yet."

"I'm so sorry. Can you talk about it?" Sometimes Jicho could tell me everything about a vision. Other times, he needed to wait until a certain thing was said or done before he could share anything.

"No." Jicho jabbed at the ground with extra force. "Can't tell you."

"Is there anything I can do?"

Jicho finally looked up to me, and I saw an old soul look out from his young eyes. "You must promise me one thing."

"Go on."

"If someone ever asked you to stop speaking to me, swear that you'd never take that vow."

I frowned. "Is this part of your vision?" What situation would possibly arise where I'd be asked to refuse Jicho's friendship? Nothing came to mind at the moment, but I set the thought aside to contemplate later.

Jicho shrugged. "Maybe."

"No, I would never take a vow like that."

"That's good." Jicho stared back at the ground once again.

My poor Jicho. Whatever this vision was, it must be quite a burden.

Rowan stepped up to the mouth of the alley. A crowd of villagers stood behind him, their silhouettes outlined by the darkened sky. "Midnight is almost here," said Rowan. "Almost time to summon Mlinzi and Walinzi." Rowan's gaze locked on Jicho. "There you are."

Jicho forced a smile, but there was no joy in it. "Hello."

"Do you want to show us your metal boat?" asked Rowan. "There's time before the ceremony starts. After that, I'm afraid all the children will be heading off to bed."

Normally, Jicho would have a number of expected responses to statements like this. First, he'd leap up with excitement to show us his new project. Second, he'd insist that he was old enough to stay up with the adults.

But Jicho did neither of these things. He merely angled his body farther away. "I'm fine. I'll stay right here. I just need a little time to myself."

Rowan's gaze intensified. "If you're certain."

"I am.:

I slipped up to Rowan's side, taking care to speak in a voice that the partygoers wouldn't hear. Not that they could hear much over the music and song. "I'm not sure we should leave Jicho."

"My brother has moods because of his visions. If he needs time to come to terms with what he's seen, then it's best to give him that."

I hugged my elbows. It felt wrong to leave the boy here. Still, Rowan had known Jicho all his life—and it was almost midnight—so this was the best I could do for now.

The sense of foreboding was still heavy on my shoulders as we headed back to the great cliff wall and its monkey sculptures. Bands of moonlight drifted over the dancing figures. Sometimes it seemed as if the monkey gods were laughing. A moment later, it looked as if they weren't dancing so much as racing toward us, baring their teeth to attack.

Rowan led me to the base of the cliff wall. "Care to cast with me again?"

"I'd love it. What's the spell?"

"It's my role to cast a summoning here. The monkeys might show up without it, but the Casters love watching my spellwork. Plus, I throw in some magickal animals for extra effect." He winked. "My people have a mage king. They expect some razzle-dazzle every so often."

I loved the mischievous glint in his eyes. "In that case, I'll have to add something to the event as well."

"I'd expect nothing less."

Rowan raised his arms and the Casters around us fell silent. After that, my mate pulled Caster magick into himself, making the veins in his right arm glow red. I did the same with Necromancer power, stopping once the bones in my left hand shone blue. The crowd around us quickly grew to a mighty throng. After all the music and laughter, the quiet suddenly became a palpable thing.

Rowan raised his arms and spoke his incantation.

Bring me the tree of life.

Oh, how I envied the shortness of Caster spells. Rowan lowered his hands. Instantly, a small pool of red haze appeared before his feet. The crimson mist quickly ballooned upward, taking the form of a great jungle tree. Long ghostly fronds arched from the top of the cliff wall to the ground around us. A great tree of life formed from red smoke.

I pursed my lips. "Not too bad."

Rowan gave me a lopsided smile. "Your turn."

Now, I knew precisely the spell to cast. Enough Necromancer power had now pooled in my left palm. Releasing it, I spoke the words of my own spell.

Life from death
Lodger from host
Summon jungle spirits
Fill this home with ghosts

A small cloud of blue smoke appeared on the ground. Within this indigo haze, a pack of blue monkey ghosts appeared. No less than fifty of them took to scaling Rowan's cloud-tree while chattering to each other and swinging from the branches. The crowd let out a satisfying chorus of gasps.

Rowan's brows lifted. "Well done."

"Thank you." I snapped my fingers, making my ghost monkeys turn silent. "We're all ready for your speech now."

"Sure you don't want to join in?" Rowan's face said he already knew the answer to this question. Once I officially became Genesis Regina, I'd have to give speeches at major occasions. Public speaking wasn't my favorite pastime, which was yet another reason not to rush into being queen.

I winked. "Positive."

"In that case..." Rowan then raised his arms once more. "My people." The silence once again became absolute. "Tonight, Elea and I celebrate the Festival of Monkeys. This is the finest celebration of the year!"

The crowd erupted in a deafening cheer. Every week, Rowan announced another festival the greatest of the year without cracking a smile. How he managed it was quite a mystery. But he did. Every time.

Rowan waved his arms, and the mass of people became silence once more. "Tonight, we celebrate our special role as Casters. We call upon magick to build our world, tap into life, and keep each other strong. At the festival of Mlinzi and Walinzi, we ask these gods to answer our summons to enhance something in our lives. Strong individuals make for a healthy community. Mlinzi and Walinzi have always been drawn to our unique kind of power. Tonight, at the appearance of the Martyr's Comet, the veil between our worlds is at its thinnest. Now let us call out our desires for our homes, families, and people. Let your voices be heard!"

From every direction, Casters begin to call out requests.

"My son is a Changed One. He's missing. Help us find him."

"Take the pain from my back."

"All I need is a small bag of gold."

"My wife and I hope for a baby."

Beside me, Rowan cupped his hand by his mouth. "I seek the Sword of Theodora."

A deep groaning sounded, the unique crash of stone against stone. Orange light glittered over the carvings on the mountainside. Magick was being cast, and since it was orange? This wasn't like anything we had in this realm. The carvings of Mlinzi and Walinzi began to move as if alive. No question about it: Mlinzi and Walinzi had cast a spell on their carved counterparts. These living images began to scan the crowd.

Rowan grinned. "That's a good sign," he said to me. "It means they will grant one wish this year. According to the archives, the carvings don't always start to move." He took in a deep breath and called in a louder voice. "I seek the Sword of Theodora."

I took up the same cry. "Help us find the Sword of Theodora!" As I called out the words, memories flooded my mind. First, I pictured the dolly-mech of the Not-Elea. After that, I recalled my gateway visions of the Sire and Lady. The question tumbled from my lips on a whisper. "And how do we use hybrid magick to heal the gateways?"

At that moment, the monkey carvings stilled. Bit by bit, their gazes shifted until both of them turned in my direction, their eyes glowing with orange light. The crowd fell silent once more.

The representations of Mlinzi and Walinzi began to speak. Their voices—one male and one female—boomed through the deepening night. "Once every two millennia, we hear the pleas of the Caster people. At these great occasions, one request may be granted. This time it shall be you, Elea of Braddock. Viktor will raise an army of Changed Ones. You must stop him with the Sword of Theodora."

The crowd gasped. All of a sudden, thousands of eyes were locked on me, expressions of terror brightening their faces. Viktor had taken the strongest Caster mages and turned them into combinations of human and animal. Changed Ones. Although we'd banished Viktor into exile, the Casters still feared him stealing away their families. Plus, more and more villages of Changed Ones had gone missing.

In other words, while I was certainly glad that Mlinzi and Walinzi had granted my wish, I certainly did not appreciate the fact that they'd discussed Viktor and his army with the general populace. Rowan and I had been trying to keep our efforts to defeat Viktor quiet for now. No one had known he would return.

Guess that was over now. By dawn, every Caster on the continent would be in a panic over Viktor's approaching army.

I steeled my resolve. Rowan and I could calm the Casters. What we needed was that damnable Sword.

A series of ear-splitting cracks sounded. The base of the cliff wall split. Orange light glistened around the new seam. A thin opening appeared in the cliff base, a passage leading into the darkness beyond.

"Enter our gateway," said Mlinzi and Walinzi. "Your questions will be answered."

I laced my fingers with Rowan's. His hands felt warm and calloused. As a spy, Rowan had entered many dangerous situations like this one. And as my mate, it helped to simply have his love and strength close by.

Rowan's gaze met mine. "We can do this."

I gave his hand a squeeze. "I believe you."

Moving in unison, we took a step closer to the newly formed entrance at the base of the cliff wall. The giant carvings of Mlinzi and Walinzi let out an angry hiss.

"Elea comes alone," they said. "Or not at all."

My blood chilled. Facing them by myself? That seemed like a terrible idea. I turned to Rowan. "Perhaps there's another way."

"We know the Sword in hidden in two parts," said Rowan. "It would be hard enough to find one piece without their help, let alone two. And since Viktor is raising an army, we don't have time for alternatives. You must go."

I nodded. Rowan was right. "I'll do my best."

"You'll succeed, Elea. I have every faith in you."

Warmth and joy spread through my chest. Going up on tiptoe, I wrapped my arms about Rowan's neck, pulling him in for a deep kiss. Normally, this type of action would cause the Casters to whoop in celebration. Now, we were met by perfect silence. The heavy quiet felt as ominous as a curse.

I broke the kiss. "I'll be back as quickly as I can."

Rowan pressed his forehead against mine. "Remember, Mlinzi and Walinzi may be tricksters, but you are more than their match. Necromancers have great skill with word games. It's not a Caster ability."

Rowan was working to build up my confidence, and I loved him for it. I wanted to tell him a thousand things: How much I adored him and his people...How happy I'd been these last months together...The way he'd changed my life and made the future something to look forward to. I could only whisper two words: "Thank you."

Turning, I began the slow march toward the cliff wall. In the growing darkness, I could see the outline of a bright orange gateway gleaming at its base. The Casters stepped away as I walked by, lining up to form a makeshift passageway. An elderly woman reached out her winkled hand to mine.

"Viktor took my grandbaby when he was only nine. Fight for us."

My eyes stung. I couldn't imagine someone kidnapping Jicho, let alone experimenting on him and turning that innocence into a weapon. I reached out tentatively, my hand shaking. Our fingertips brushed as I stepped past. My mouth twitched with held-in emotions. I was no expert at speech making. The touch would have to be enough.

I stepped forward. Another hand reached out.

"My mother is a Changed One."

And again.

"My best friend was taken."

I reached out, brushing my fingertips against theirs. Suddenly, all the Casters on either side of the makeshift passageway were reaching out to me. Rough whispers echoed through the night air.

"My village has disappeared."

"Our Changed Ones are vanishing."

"Protect them."

"Save us."

Tears streamed down my cheeks. Crying was forbidden by Necromancers—it was a sign that we'd lost control of our emotions. But I couldn't seem to stop my tears.

These sad souls. So many had lost friends and family to Viktor, and now I was their last hope to protect their loved ones.

I closed in on the glowing orange gateway with one thought on my mind: this simply had to work. For all of us.

CHAPTER SEVEN

Lowering my arms, I walked through the opening the rock wall and entered a dark tunnel. A spine-rattling boom sounded behind me as the cliff face magickally sewed itself together behind me.

I was trapped now. There was no returning to the Caster village.

The tunnel became so quiet, the sound of my own breath turned deafening. The darkness around me seemed almost absolute. I spun about, my footfalls sloshing on the wet cave floor. A faint glimmer reflected off the water—a light shone up ahead. I blinked hard as my vision adjusted. Surely, I could cast a spell for brightness, but I wanted to save all my energy for Mlinzi and Walinzi. Who knew what would happen once I met them?

With every passing second, my vision grew sharper. I scanned the walls around me. The passage appeared to be rough-hewn from a massive chunk of natural stone. For years, I had studied Necromancy at the Zelle Cloister, a place that had literally been scraped out of a mountain by skeletal servants. I knew a carved passageway when I saw one.

I followed the faint glimmer on the water. Soon the tunnel grew brighter. More sounds echoed in as well. I could make out the unmistakable growl of predators, the bright caws of birds, and the low chitter of insects. This combination of noise was something else I was quite familiar with—the unmistakable sounds of a jungle. What better place to greet monkey gods?

I followed the growing light and sound until I reached another archway. In the space beneath the arch wound lines of orange light.

Magick.

This was another gateway. But to where?

Holding my breath, I stepped into the net of orange light.

For a moment, it felt as if every fiber of my body was being torn apart. Orange and yellow lights flashed around me. The scent of charcoal and blood filled my senses.

The next thing I knew, I was standing in the most unusual jungle I'd ever seen. In some ways, the place resembled the lands around Rowan's castle. Palm trees stood tall, vines dangling from their wide fronds. Long-beaked birds swooped between the trunks. Insects crept along the muddy earth below them. Humidity and heat pressed onto my skin.

That was where there similarities ended, though. Here, the entire place was colored in shades of orange. There were tangerine-colored birds and bright amber insects. A pale citrine sky arched overhead. Two great orange suns cast a colored glow. The scent of overripe flowers filled the air.

Plus, everything here was sized on a massive scale. The trees towered mountain-high before me. Orange ants skittered by in a neat row, all of them tall enough to reach my knees. I'd never seen anything like it.

For a few seconds, it was all I could to soak in the world around me. After that, a pair of massive orange monkeys dropped onto the ground nearby. *Mlinzi and Walinzi.* When I finally gave them my full attention, it was with the realization that if these gods wished to, one of them could easily squash me underfoot.

"He-hello," I stammered.

"I'm Mlinzi," said the first monkey. He had a deep voice and a long tail that lashed behind him with a predatory air.

"I'm Walinzi," said the second. She scanned me with wide and compassionate eyes.

"Thank you for agreeing to help me."

Mlinzi stared me like I was the main entrée at lunch. He grinned, showing a mouth of pointed teeth. "You'll need the Sword of Theodora and soon."

"Viktor will raise his army against you," added Walinzi. "A great battle is coming." She tilted her head and stared at me with pinprick eyes in her amber face. Unlike Mlinzi, Walinzi seemed to regard me as an object of sad interest versus a main course of food.

Rowan's warnings echoed in my mind. "You're trickster gods," I said. "How do I know this isn't all an illusion?"

Mlinzi merely licked his lips slowly. "You don't."

Walinzi swatted him on the shoulder. "Don't mind my brother. He has no taste for anything but eating."

"Excellent point," said Mlinzi. "This one could be rather tasty."

Walinzi huffed out a breath. "You promised not to eat any more of my little projects."

Mlinzi smile grew impossibly broad. "I break promises all the time."

It was good that I had years of Necromancer training, because it taught me to control my emotions. Right now, my instincts were screaming for me to run. After all, a massive orange monkey was staring at me like he was about to munch on my arm for a snack. But I didn't take Mlinzi so much for a hunter as a bully. He wanted to see me quiver with fear. I wouldn't give him the satisfaction.

Instead, I focused my attention on Walinzi. She seemed the more reasonable of the two. "I'm here as you requested. I appreciate your offer of help. Where can I find the Sword of Theodora?"

"That's your first question?" Walinzi squealed with joy while hopping up and down, making the ground rumble beneath my feet. It was an extremely animal-like display for someone who seemed so logical just a few moments ago.

"She doesn't know anything," said Mlinzi. "How is that the case?"

Walinzi stopped her happy jumping. "I told you, the Sire and Lady are fools."

My heart thudded faster in my chest, and not just from the instinct to flee. "What do you mean? Where is the Sword?"

"That's one question we can answer for you, and we will... Eventually." Walinzi grinned. "Let's not forget you had another question as well. You were asking us about hybrid magick and gateways."

Mlinzi bared his teeth. "Yes, you need to know how to heal your realm without dying."

The words tumbled from my mouth, seemingly on their own. "Of course, I want to know. Very much so."

"In that case, we can help you with both questions," said Walinzi. "But we have our price."

"And what is that?" I asked.

"You'll find out soon enough," said Walinzi. "First, you must look behind you."

I didn't move. Mlinzi and Walinzi could just tell me where to find the Sword and the how to wield hybrid magick, but they were already playing games. My fingers itched to cast a spell. In theory, a Compulsion would force them to answer my questions, but in reality? They appeared far too powerful to be affected.

No question about it. This was going to be a game of wits, not magick.

Turning around, I examined the rock wall that I'd just stepped out of. Set into the surface was a series of massive orange gemstones, all of them neatly aligned into a familiar arch shape.

A gateway to a new land. That gave me an idea. These two trickster gods needed to see me as more than a meal or pet project. I had knowledge as well that I could put into play here.

Turning about, I refocused on Mlinzi and Walinzi. "I see your gateway. Is this your means of letting me know my world connects to others? I'm aware. I also know that the Sire and Lady happen to rule those worlds, including yours. Do you see them as tyrants, by chance?"

"Tyrants? TYRANTS!" Mlinzi pounded the earth with his massive fists. The ground shook with the force of his fury.

Walinzi leaned forward until her snout was inches from my face. "We're different from all those other worlds in the Meadow of Many Gateways. We aren't controlled by the Sire and Lady."

Mlinzi hopped with rage. "Oo-oo-oooo!"

My mind raced through this information. "So you're helping me in the hopes that I defeat the Sire and Lady somehow?"

Mlinzi stopped moving. His eyes flared with orange light. "Yes. Keep us free."

"And that's why you'll tell me how to recharge the gateways."

Mlinzi kept hopping with rage. "No healing the gateways! No, no, no!"

"You don't want the gateways healed? But that would destroy my world. I can't allow that to happen."

"NO HEALING!"

While Mlinzi kept railing, Walinzi merely tilted her head, staring at me with new intensity. "You're a clever one, aren't you? We see things, my brother and I."

"You have the gift of foresight."

Walinzi casually picked nits from her fur. "We see things. Different visions and futures than you do, but we have foresight, yes. Sometimes we use our gifts to—how do I put this?—cause the Sire and Lady trouble."

"Tricksters."

"More than tricks this time," howled Mlinzi. "You can save us. You can free us all! Kill the Sire and Lady with the Sword."

I held my arms up with my palms forward. "If I get the Sword of Theodora, then I'll use it to kill Viktor, but only if he attacks. The same is true for the Sire and Lady. If you want them dead, I won't do your dirty work."

Walinzi clacked her teeth together in quick succession. "Do not be too quick to judge what you will do."

"I am not killing any gods for you."

Mlinzi grabbed handfuls of muddy earth and flung them aside. "Kill! Kill!"

"Killing is not required," said Walinzi. "We simply ask for our freedom. And no matter what happens, you must know we're on your side."

My eyes narrowed. "I didn't realize there were sides."

Mlinzi paused, his fists overflowing with earth. "That's your biggest problem, Elea of Braddock. You're a fool. Of course, there are sides."

"Our help will not be what you expect," said Walinzi. "However, it shall be what you require."

My stomach sunk to my toes. I'd heard statements like this from Petra before, right before she locked me up and tried to force me to become Tsarina. "In other words," I said slowly, "I'm going to hate whatever you do next."

Walinzi nudged Mlinzi with her massive elbow. "See? I told you this one was intelligent. She understands." Walinzi fell forward onto her arms, setting the ground shaking again. "Our help will not come easily. But without us, you will never find the Sword of Theodora or learn how to use hybrid magick. Are you willing to bargain with us?"

Her huge orange face loomed before me. It took everything in me not to flinch or run away. However, I stayed focused on the images of so many Casters reaching out to me as I headed into the gateway. Those people deserved answers and peace. So did I. "Name your price."

Walinzi's eyes flared orange and bright. "You must never see Jicho again or communicate with him in any way."

My back teeth locked. Jicho had said something about this before, back in the alley at the festival. I promised the boy I would always speak to him. *Had Jicho foreseen this moment?* If so, it wasn't very good news. When Jicho warned me, he hadn't been in the best of moods. Still, I wouldn't go back on my promise.

When I spoke again, I kept my body stiff and straight in true Necromancer fashion. "Absolutely not. Name another price."

After this, there was a lot of hopping about and screeching, both from Mlinzi and Walinzi. The pair swung from long orange vines, their claw-like toes almost taking off my skull as they swooped overhead. The entire time, I kept my face passive and my stance strong. I couldn't let them see that they'd unnerved me, even though my heart was thudding so hard in my chest, I thought it might break free to clog up my throat.

"Are you quite through?" I asked.

At length, Mlinzi and Walinzi stopped their display and sat before me once more. Mlinzi bared his pointed teeth again. "Perhaps this one is too clever," he growled.

Walinzi scrambled behind her brother and began pawing at his shoulder. "Let's see…Another form of payment." She paused. "Perhaps you could give us a memory."

"A memory, yes." Mlinzi orange eyes locked on me. "That will work well."

A chill ran up my torso. Before, I'd had a sense of how the tricksters where playing their games. Now, I wasn't so certain. "What kind of memory will you take, good or bad?"

Walinzi shrugged. "That's all in one's point of view, isn't it?"

"That's not what I meant. Will taking these memories hurt anyone?"

"No one will be injured," said Mlinzi.

I frowned. There was a trick in here, but I couldn't see it. "There are many definitions of injury," I said.

Walinzi's wide orange eyes became even larger. "We can only protect from physical harm," she said. "We gods don't understand how your kind feels about every little thing."

"And you'll get the memory back after you succeed," added Mlinzi.

Rubbing my neck, I thought through these conditions. Mlinzi and Walinzi probably did have a rather hazy view of human emotions. Having them promise no injury was about as good as I could secure.

"I must say, this is a rather fine bargain." Walinzi stopped fussing with her brother and hopped closer to me. "Do you want the Sword or not?"

"We've only spoken about the Sword," I countered. "What about the secret of how to heal the gateways with hybrid magick? You promised that as well."

"Gateways are evil," growled Mlinzi. "No healing."

"Evil or not, I need information about both the gateways and the Sword."

Walinzi pursed her long lips. "And you may have both."

I frowned. This negotiation was going far too easily. These two tricksters were up to something. "And you'll give me all of that—both the Sword and the way to heal the gateways—in exchange for one memory."

"Not exactly." Walinzi raised a pair of fingers. "It would be two memories then."

I suppressed a smile. We were negotiating terms now, and that was far more comfortable ground for me. "And for those two memories, I would get both the Sword and the way to heal the gateways with hybrid magick…without my dying in the process." It was always very important to be clear in a negotiation.

"Yes, yes." Walinzi rolled her eyes as if my clarifying were the silliest thing she'd ever encountered. I didn't believe her act for a second.

"I want those memories back after I get the Sword."

"Ungrateful little witch," growled Mlinzi.

"Both memories."

"Fine, fine," said Walinzi. The satisfied gleam shone in her eyes. I didn't like that look at all. It was as if I was about to make a huge error, and Walinzi couldn't believe her good fortune.

An image popped into my mind—something from my talk with Amelia back at the lab. The Sword was in two pieces. "I want one memory for all parts of the Sword." Perhaps there were more than two pieces.

Walinzi huffed. "That's rather unreasonable. The Sword is in two pieces now. It could break down even more. We need one memory for each part of the Sword. Our services aren't free, you know."

So this was their game. Who knew how many memories they planned to take? If I weren't careful, I might end up leaving here without knowing my own name. "Two memories for *all* parts of the Sword of Theodora *and* the secret of how to heal the gateways." With this statement, Mlinzi and Walinzi began to hop around, so I raised my hand, palm forward. "And please, don't bother to jump about in another display. A simple yes or no will do."

The monkey gods ceased their jumping. It was a good thing, too, since all the movement was making me seasick. Mlinzi looked at his sister expectantly. For her part, Walinzi drummed her long fingers on her kneecaps for a few long moments. At last, she spoke again. "This is a horrid bargain, but yes, we agree to taking four memories for the Sword and truth."

"Two memories."

Walinzi tapped her chin. "Did I say four?"

"You did. It's two."

"My sister and I agree," said Mlinzi. "Do you?"

I couldn't believe the pair of them weren't still trying to pull some kind of verbal trick on me. I narrowed my eyes. "And those memories will return after I find the Sword?"

"Yes," said Walinzi smoothly. "And no one will be injured by the memories' disappearance."

My mind spun through every angle and loophole. I couldn't find one. I'd made it clear that I wouldn't be killing any gods for Mlinzi and Walinzi...And I did still need the Sword. "In that case, I agree."

Mlinzi whooped, making more "oo-oo-ooo" noises. A low boom of thunder rolled over the jungle. The atmosphere became thick with the charged sense of magick. Black clouds appeared, covering up the pale orange sky. Mlinzi and Walinzi were about to cast their spell, and whatever it was, it would be huge.

Every instinct I had told me to cower. I couldn't, though. I'd gotten this far without being seen as weak; I simply had to keep my features calm.

Suddenly, orange lighting bolts jutted down from the clouds. One by one, they formed a circle around me. Instead of a quick flash, each bolt remained in an arc that dug into the ground, churning up stones and earth as it let off shower of tiny sparks. More and more of these little points of light filled the air, until I couldn't see anything else. The sparks then settled on my skin, but they didn't burn me. It took everything I had not to scream.

At this point, I considered that fact an accomplishment. Soon the sparks covered me in a glowing sheen of orange-hued brightness.

A pair of lightning bolts flashed right into my eyes. I could almost feel the sparkling fingers rooting around my head, finding the two memories, and ripping them out. My head turned woozy. White spots filled my vision. A sheen of sweat broke out over my skin. *What memories were taken from me?*

"Enough," cried Mlinzi and Walinzi together.

The sparks faded. The lightning bolts fully burrowed into the earth, disappearing from view. The dark clouds rolled away. Once again, two suns burned in a pale orange sky. Mlinzi and Walinzi had cast a spell without using incantations. *Interesting.* Magick must work differently in this world.

I looked down to find myself wearing my Necromancer robes. These were ones that marked me as a Grand Mistress. I frowned. What were they up to? They wouldn't change my clothing without a purpose.

"What memories did you take from me?" I gestured across my robes. "And why am I dressed this way?"

"You're clever enough to figure that out on your own," said Walinzi. "Eventually."

I scanned my thoughts. I could remember growing up on Braddock Farm, learning Necromancy at the Zelle Cloister, and falling in love with Rowan. What else could be important? For the first time since I arrived in this strange place, I felt as if I could breathe freely. Perhaps these monkey gods were truly enemies of the Sire and Lady. The price was possibly the memory of some random flower or esoteric spell.

Only, Mlinzi and Walinzi didn't seem like the types to make it that easy. I sighed. Soon enough, I'm sure I'd discover their full plan. "Now, tell me where the Sword may be found, as well as how to heal the gateways."

Mlinzi let out a series of loud whoops. "Not yet! Not yet!"

"What my brother means to say is that we have more to tell you," explained Walinzi. "To find the Sword, you must first seek out the exiled Necromancers. Find your friend Nan. She can help you locate the Sword's hilt, as well as give you information about the Sire and Lady."

I knew Walinzi had said many things, but all I could focus on was the name Nan. She'd been my friend while I'd been cursed. Agents of the Tsar had killed her.

"How can that help me?" I asked. "Nan is dead."

"Oh, no. Far from it." Walinzi chuckled, and I thought she was enjoying this far too much. *Trickster.* "Your Nan is alive and waiting for you. You didn't know this because she doesn't trust you enough to tell."

I pictured Nan's smiling face. She and I had been imprisoned at the Midnight Cloister so the evil Mother Superior, Marlene, could drain our power for Viktor's use. No matter how horrible things became, Nan always had a sunny outlook and a plan. It would be wonderful to see her again. But why wouldn't she trust me?

"That's why we gave you the robes," added Mlinzi. "Now you're dressed properly to greet your friend." He smiled more widely than ever, showing his mouth of extra-sharp canines. "And we did all that for free."

Walinzi fanned herself. "We're regular philanthropists."

I didn't believe that for a second. "And where will I find Nan, exactly?" I could cast a divining spell to get the precise location, but I was curious what the monkey gods would say.

"Ha," called Walinzi. "That's for you to discover." She gestured back toward the arch in the mountainside. "You can return to your world through that gateway." She rocked back and forth while chittering happily. "You're quite the clever girl."

Mlinzi face rounded into a smile that could only be described as evil. "Clever, clever girl." The words made my insides twist with worry. They both seemed far too pleased with themselves.

"But what about the spell for healing the gateways? You haven't said a thing about that."

"This will aid you," said Walinzi. An orange light flared on my hand. When it vanished, I found that my mating band had been transformed into an orange ring carved with the image of Mlinzi and Walinzi. *Another totem ring.* This was beyond belief. I raised my hand. "You took away my mating band and gave me your totem ring? What does this do?"

"You'll see," said Walinzi. "It will prove crucial."

I stared at the band with new interest. "Will this ring help me heal the gateways?"

"No." Walinzi rolled her eyes. "First, you must find the Sword. Once you have that weapon in hand, you'll know how to heal the gateways."

"Sword first," called Mlinzi. "Remember that. Sword first and gateways second."

I pressed my palms against my eyes. "That's not as specific as what I'd hoped for."

Without saying another word, Mlinzi and Walinzi leapt up into trees and disappeared from view. The only sign that I'd seen them was the torn-up earth by my feet. What had Walinzi called me?

Clever girl.

All of a sudden, I didn't feel quite so clever at all. Mlinzi and Walinzi both seemed far too happy with our bargain, especially because they'd already betrayed me by only giving me half of what I need. *That can't be a good thing.*

Still, I wasn't sure what other choice I had. Mlinzi, Walinzi, and Jicho all agreed that Viktor was soon to arrive with an enemy army. There was nothing for it but to return to my own world and find the Sword of Theodora, as well as the truth about the Sire and Lady. I'd driven the best bargain I could.

Now, there was nothing left to do but go back through the gateway and hope for the best.

CHAPTER EIGHT

As I approached the gateway, the same strings of orange power formed a webwork under the open archway. I winced, remembering how it had hurt to pass through last time. Even so, I wouldn't let a little pain keep me in this world. Needless to say, I didn't trust Mlinzi and Walinzi.

I stepped past the gateway and felt the same overwhelming pain as before. Gritting my teeth, I walked into the darkened tunnel beyond. The pain vanished. Excitement sped my steps. My Necromancer training told me to keep my hopes tamped down, but I couldn't help it. I felt like shouting my successes.

I'd found my first clue to finding the Sword!

Sure, I didn't know how to heal the gateways yet, but once I found the Sword, I'd discover that next. If nothing else, I had a plan. And even better, Nan was alive.

Smiling, I stepped out of the tunnel and into the outskirts of the Caster village. The moment I stepped away from the cliff wall, a slab of stone rolled down from the hidden depths above me, blocking my way back to Mlinzi and Walinzi. That didn't worry me too much, though. I was in no rush to spend more time with those two.

The moment I emerged, everything stopped. Meats ceased to be turned on their spits. Dancers paused. Somewhere, a flute player dropped their instrument with a loud clang. A beam of moonlight seemed to brighten the spot where I stood as if I were standing in a slice of daylight.

Strange. I was certain that the Caster people had been getting used to me. And the way they'd reached out as I entered the cliff wall before? I was sure we'd connected in far deeper ways. Then, I remembered my Necromancer robes.

That's right, I'd changed clothes.

Most Casters had never seen me in Necromancer garb. Perhaps that's what had upset them. Also, I'd just stepped off into another realm to discover if I could find the Sword of Theodora, the only weapon that could protect these people from Viktor. The knew his army was coming. Of course, they'd be anxious about what had happened.

I scanned the crowd and quickly spotted Rowan standing beside one of the smaller bonfires. He looked the same as before: tall and handsome with his long cloak, bare chest, and leather trousers. Even though he'd decided not to wear his crown tonight, there was no mistaking who was king in this place. Joy soared through my soul. Forgetting everything else, I rushed over to stand before my mate.

"Rowan, I have excellent news." I pitched my voice loud so all the crowd could hear. After all, that was why they were quietly staring anyway. And since my mission had been successful, there was no reason to whisper. "I met Mlinzi and Walinzi. They have told me where to find the Sword of Theodora, just as we'd hoped."

Rowan merely stared at me, his intense green gaze scanning me from head to toe. Despite the jungle heat, a chill of foreboding crept up my back. I remembered my Necromancer robes.

I pulled on my black skirt. "In case you're wondering, Mlinzi and Walinzi changed my dress for me. They even changed out my mating band into a totem ring." I checked out Rowan's hand.

Sure enough, they had changed his as well. Instead of a mating band, he now wore a simple ring made of orange-colored metal. "Your mating band is gone as well. That's terrible."

Rowan kept staring and not speaking. Maybe I needed to make things more clear.

"They did all this because they want me to find Nan." I forced a smile. "You remember Nan? I told you about her. She helped me escape the Midnight Cloister."

Rowan's gaze turned even more intense. My skin broke out into gooseflesh. On reflex, my hand went to my throat. "What happened while I was gone? Is everyone all right?"

At last, Rowan broke the silence. "I don't know who you are or how you got here, but Necromancers are not welcome on our lands. Not after what your Tsar Viktor did to our people. Did you think you could simply walk in and spy on my subjects?"

Shock tingled through every inch of my body. I knew my mate. There was no mistaking the corded muscles in his neck. Rowan was enraged. Had he enjoyed the party too much while I was gone? I'd seen other Casters grow unreasonable with drink, but Rowan was never one to partake.

"What are you talking about?" I asked. "Have you been at the berry wine?" I swiped the cup from his hand and sniffed at it. It was water. "Was this tested before you drank from it?" There had been attempted poisonings in the past. Even though Viktor was in exile, he had followers in both the Casters and Necromancers. I wouldn't put it past any of them to try to drug my mate.

Rowan stared at me as if I were coated in poison myself. "Kade! Bring the guard."

"Yes, I should very much like to see Kade." Rowan's brother was always honest. The rest of the Casters might be too frightened to stand up to their king when his mind was gone, but not Kade.

Kade broke through the crowd. Rowan's brother froze when he saw me. His features slumped with disbelief. "How did a Necromancer get in here?"

Fresh waves of shock poured through my limbs. Kade didn't know who I was? What was going on? My heart sank. A question appeared. What if the memories Mlinzi and Walinzi had stolen weren't mine?

No, no, no. There had to be another explanation.

Rowan's features stayed intense. "And this one is a Grand Mistress to boot." His mouth twisted with disgust. "If you tell us what you know of Viktor, I promise you a quick death. You have my word on it."

My mind reeled. Kade didn't know who I was, either. *And Rowan wanted me dead?* The reality of what happened loomed larger in my mind, but I simply couldn't give up too easily. I had to be missing something here. When I spoke again, my voice was a hoarse whisper. "You know me. I'm Elea."

Jicho broke through the crowd next. I'd never been happier to see his bald head and red robes. His brown eyes were bright with fear. "I know her!" He pointed right at me. "I saw her in a vision. Don't hurt her. She's here to help us."

"Jicho?" My voice shook with relief. "You know me?"

The boy nodded. "The first memory they took. It wasn't yours; it was all the Casters', except for me."

His words slammed into me like so many fireball spells. My worst suspicions were true. *None of the Caster people knew who I was any more. Not even Rowan.* My stomach lurched. The thought of losing my mate made me ill.

Amelia burst out from the crowd. She was still wearing her pink Caster leathers. Her gaze scanned Kade, Rowan, Jicho, and me. She instantly moved to stand before Jicho, creating a physical barrier between the Seer boy and me.

"Jicho, stay back," warned Amelia. "She's a Grand Mistress Necromancer. Don't let her cast a spell on you."

My legs turned wobbly beneath me. Clearly, Amelia didn't know who I was, either. The spell must have registered her as a Caster now. It made sense, considering how she was mated to Kade. It just was a terrible turn of events.

"She won't hurt us." Jicho popped his head out from behind Amelia. "I told you, I had a vision. You can't make her talk about Viktor or his plans. She's has nothing of value to tell you. You'll only be torturing and murdering her for nothing. And we need her. I've seen it."

My breath caught. Suddenly, I'd gone from sharing my adventure with Mlinzi and Walinzi to having a nine-year old negotiate for my life. It was almost too much to follow.

Rowan shook his head. "No, Jicho. She's Viktor's spy. We must get what information we can."

Jicho ran over and pulled on his brother's hand. "Just let her go. She doesn't know anything that can help us."

Kade still stared at me as if I were a walking disease. "There's a guard tower on the other side of the village. It's well warded. We'll put her there, talk to her for a bit, and then...Let her go."

I know what Kade really means. "You still plan to interrogate and kill me."

Rowan frowned. "You knew me and Kade on sight. Our identities are closely guarded outside the Caster community. You're definitely a spy, which means you realized the threat of being captured, and yet you walked right into my festival."

"I'm not a spy, unlike some." I gave him glare for glare. When it was needed, Rowan was a skilled spymaster for his people. "All I want to do is speak with Jicho and leave, but without being tortured, questioned, or killed. Give me your word that you will do this, and I'll go to your tower without causing trouble."

"How do I know I can trust you, Necromancer?" He stared pointedly at my left hand.

"Because I already know I can trust you. You're a man of your word. Plus, I know you won't believe this, but I'm your mate." My voice cracked as I said the word *mate*.

Amelia shook her head. "Perhaps she's gone insane, poor thing."

Rowan still stared at me, but the tension was gone from his neck. I was starting to make him wonder. "Fine. You have my word that you'll be safe and unharmed. But you will go to the tower without trouble. One misstep and our deal will become forfeit."

"Agreed." I didn't add that no matter what wards Kade thought were in that tower, I could probably break through them easily.

"And you." Rowan turned to Jicho. "If I catch you anywhere near this spy, I'll lock you up in the Seer temple for a week. I mean it."

Jicho folded his skinny arms over his thin chest. "You're terrible."

A stricken look crossed Rowan's face. It was too fast for others to catch, but I knew my mate. I focused on Jicho. "Don't be too hard on your brother. He only wants to protect you."

Kade's mouth twisted into a sneer. "We better be careful with this one. She's a born manipulator."

Rowan's gaze locked with mine. "This one... She's..." Something in his eyes softened. Was our mate bond still in place? Did he still feel something for me?

I couldn't help the note of hope in my voice. "Yes? I'm what?"

The gentle look on Rowan's face melted into a scowl. "You're nothing to me. Take her to the tower. The one in the northwest quadrant."

"Northwest?" asked Kade.

"That's what I ordered," replied Rowan. "And be sure she has no missteps along the way."

A light of understanding flashed in Kade's eyes. "As you command."

My thoughts ran through everything they'd said. There was some plot afoot about locking me in this particular tower.

Good fortune with that plan. I was still a Grand Mistress Necromancer, and I would escape.

Kade and another half dozen guards stepped forward and walked me toward one of the towers on the outskirts of the village. Sure enough, the wards grew stronger as we approached the structure, but even so, these spells were minor. I'd broken through far worse wards with ease. I could do the same here.

Kade led me up the winding tower steps, opened a small wooden door, and gestured for me to walk inside. I stepped into the small round chamber. It held little more than a pallet stuffed with straw.

"Prepare to stay here for some time," said Kade. "Rowan may have promised not to hurt you, but I said no such thing. You know how many Caster families were destroyed by your master's experiments?"

I hugged my elbows. "I do. That's why I've been working to get the Sword of Theodora. Viktor will attack again, and when he does, the man must die. And by getting the Sword, Mlinzi and Walinzi say I'll learn how to save myself from the prophecy of the Martyr's Comet. That's even more reason to defeat Viktor."

"What a clever manipulator you are. Don't bother to weave your lies around me. I know the truth. You're a spy from that fiend. It will be my pleasure to introduce you to a new level of pain."

The speech was meant to frighten me, but it didn't work. I planned to transport from this spot well before the sun rose. Plus, this kind of threat was merely Kade being protective and over-bearing. I understood that he only wanted to keep his family safe. It made sense to try to interrogate me before leaving.

He'd learn to live with disappointment.

"I understand," I said.

"Good." Kade slammed the door closed and stomped away. As he moved down the steps, I heard him call out orders to the nearby guards. Evidently, I was to have a record number of warriors protecting my tower.

Now, I needed to start casting and escape. With that realization, a hollow feeling moved through my bones. I'd gotten so used to having Rowan in my life. Being without his strength and love made me feel bare.

Nothing to be done about it. If I wanted Rowan back, I needed to find the Sword of Theodora. Once I had that weapon in my possession, Rowan's memories would return. At this point, I didn't know which I wanted more: to protect Rowan from Viktor's armies, or to see him look upon me with love again.

Both were essential to my soul.

CHAPTER NINE

The moment Kade left the room, I set about casting a spell. There was no question in my mind that Kade intended to interrogate me, and it wouldn't be pleasant. Even so, by the time Rowan's brother returned, I'd be long gone.

Thank you, magick.

My plan was twofold. First, I would cast a finder spell in order to discover where Nan was hiding. Second, I'd transport there. Mlinzi and Walinzi had said something about the exiled.

To find the Sword, you must seek out the exiled Necromancers.

The exiled. I suspected that was more than a random name. If my guess was right, a group of Necromancers were living outside Petra's control. The woman was out of her mind, after all. I had to imagine some of the Necromancers were clever enough to escape her insanity.

A grand escape—that sounds like exactly the kind of thing my Nan would enjoy.

My eyes stung with emotion. I never thought I'd see Nan again. She'd died back at the Midnight Cloister, thanks to the treachery of its Mother Superior. Was Nan's death some kind of ruse? Had the Sire of Souls stepped in to help? I couldn't wait to find out how she'd ended up alive. In the end, it didn't matter so long as I could see her again. The familiar lines of Nan's face flashed in my mind: ebony skin, intelligent brown eyes, and a white-toothed smile.

How I longed to see her once more.

My body hummed with a combination of excitement and worry. This was not the moment to contemplate reunions. Kade could return at any second.

I needed to cast and quickly.

Closing my eyes, I reached out with my mage senses. The surrounding area was rich in Necromancer magick. Layers of bones lay hidden in the arid ground—these made the perfect source for my kind of power. Using all my focus, I wrapped my thoughts around the power I wished to take and tried to pull that magick into my body.

I couldn't. Foreign magick stopped me. Wards.

As Kade had warned, another force lay between me and the power I sought. A webwork of ancient wards encircled the tower. These spells allowed me to reach out with ease, but blocked any magick from entering back inside. Without power in my body, I couldn't cast.

I probed the net of blocking spells about me. It wasn't wise to break spells without understanding how they worked. My consciousness spun along the threads of the webwork, checking how each functioned. These wards had been cast by a senior-level mage, but they were far too old to stop someone like me. Like any long-standing spell, wards needed to be refreshed with energy from time to time. No one had been keeping these strong.

Good for me.

Keeping the magick firm in my mind, I sent my power tearing back through the wards around the tower. I then pulled fresh magick back into me. Energy careened through my limbs until every corner of my body felt charged. Using my Necromancer

training, I sent that energy toward my hands. New magick prickled along my skin like the brush of a thousand needles. Soon, the
bones in my hands and forearms glowed with blue light.

The time had come to cast my spell. There were various kinds
of finders that I could choose from. One of the most powerful was
a Blue Oracle, a floating skull covered in sapphires that would
answer any questions. Blue Oracles could not only help pinpoint
where someone was hiding, but they would also share all the key
facts about to approach them. I opened my mouth, ready to speak
the words to the spell.

No sound came from lips.

The words to the spell simply didn't appear in my mind.

I racked my memory. There was no way I could forget this particular spell. My Mother Superior, Petra, had drilled me on it for
months. In fact, Petra kept me awake for six consecutive days
until I got the wording, tone, and intention just right. By the time
my training on this spell was over, I was reciting it in my sleep,
much to the sadness of the other elderly sisters who shared my
same dormitory room.

How could I forget those words?

I shook my head. No matter. Today had certainly been a trying
one. My true mate had just stared at me like I was a total stranger.
That would enough to make anyone forget a few things. Besides,
there were other finder spells I could cast. For example, the spell
for Rune Bones would be just as helpful. In this casting, the bones
wouldn't actually speak like the Blue Oracle, but they would spell
out words. I'd get the information I needed. It would simply take
a bit longer. *Nothing to worry about.* I took in a deep breath, ready
to say that incantation.

Again, I couldn't remember a word.

My heartbeat sped. This couldn't be right. Surely, I could
remember a single finder spell. I listed out every finder spell in the
Necromancer lexicon.

Mystic Cloud.

Orb Of Insight.

Stylus Of The Seer.

In each case, I knew the spell and how it worked, but I couldn't recall a single word of the incantations that actually made them come to pass. Panic tightened every muscle in my torso.

Stay calm, Elea. Perhaps it was just the finder spells that were giving me trouble for some reason. I then focused on basic spells any Novice could master.

Fireball.

Bone Shield.

Detect Mage.

Again, I knew what the spells were. I could remember learning them. Still, I couldn't recall a single word of the incantations that made them function. I stared at my hands, which still glowed with blue power. Pulling in magick and directing it inside my body was something that took me years to master. How could I operate as a Grand Mistress Necromancer in some ways but not in others? The answer appeared to me in a flash.

Mlinzi and Walinzi.

The trickster gods had said they would take two memories. Jicho confirmed that the first was removing knowledge of my identity from anyone in the Caster community. Was the second any memory of how to actually cast a spell?

It had to be. There was no other explanation for me losing so many incantations at once. This wasn't magick that I'd ever heard of, either from a Necromancer or a Caster. It had to be something unique created by the trickster gods.

Bands of despair tightened around my chest. Mlinzi and Walinzi left me with the power to sense magick, but took away my ability actually do something useful with it.

Tricksters, indeed.

With a sigh, I released the magick from my body. Power rolled out from my fingertips in a cascade of blue sparks. The tiny lights faded as they reentered the environment. Within seconds, the skin on my arms and hands looked normal once again.

I shook my head. I may appear normal, but I felt anything but.

Thanks to Mlinzi and Walinzi, I wasn't a regular mortal anymore, but I wasn't a mage, either. My powers were trapped someplace in between. It all seemed so useless and cruel. Perhaps the trickster gods had lied about wanting to assist me. After all, I only had their word that they felt the Sire and Lady threatened their world.

A knock sounded at the door. "May I enter?" My breath caught as I recognized the voice. *Rowan.*

An odd mixture of excitement, terror, and desire moved through me. "Come in."

Rowan pushed open the door and stepped inside. I scanned his face carefully, desperate for any sign that he recognized me as his mate. There was none. I'd learned to gauge Rowan's expressions, and the look he wore now? It said that I was nothing but an interloper and threat.

Rowan leaned against the closed door. For some reason, he'd changed out of his long cape and leather kilt. My brows lifted in surprise. Rowan always liked to face foreigners in his formal garb. But for some reason, he had changed into his typical Caster leathers, which consisted of brown pants, heavy boots, and a fitted jacket. Weapons were strapped all over his body.

Rowan stepped slowly around the space, stomping on the floorboards a few times. They creaked and swayed. This was classic Rowan. He was sizing up how well this place could hold me if I decided to physically tear the room apart. Based on how the wood crackled under his weight, the answer was obvious. This tower had not been kept well. Plus, based on how the floorboards shifted under Rowan's prodding, the place was probably originally built to store goods, not keep prisoners. No doubt, I could easily find a way out if I stayed here too long.

The thought made me pause. I remembered Rowan's words earlier.

"One misstep and our deal will become forfeit."

Was Rowan trying to set me up to betray him? Trying to escape would certainly count as a misstep. And placing me in a storage chamber instead of a prison tower was essentially inviting one.

Rowan paused at the open window-hole, inspecting the dark grounds below. "Too many guards," he murmured. "And too close to the wall."

"You want the guards farther away."

Rowan rounded on me. "Don't you?"

"You're trying to tempt me into making a misstep, just like you warned me before. Once I try to escape, you can torture and kill me without breaking your word."

"Yes, and I have every confidence you'll miss that step and soon." Rowan leaned out the window and whistled three short notes. It was one of the codes used between Kade and Rowan. In this case, Rowan was ordering his brother to send the guards away for a while.

"Consider me sorely tempted." It didn't seem wise to keep talking about being Rowan's mate. I knew how the man's mind worked. If I came on too strong, Rowan would take that as a sure sign that I was Viktor's spy.

Rowan folded his arms across his chest, a movement that made his leathers creak. "You should have been gone by now. Why are you still here?"

My mind reeled through this statement. The fact that Rowan had changed from his royal garb now made perfect sense. "You expected me to transport away from here. That's why you changed clothes. You were planning to track me." It was a good plan. By following where I went, Rowan could probably get better information than interrogation. And afterward, Rowan would be free to interrogate and kill me at his leisure.

Rowan crossed the room in a few quick strides, pausing to stand right before me. I could feel his warmth radiate over my body. "Why are you still here, Necromancer? The wards aren't strong enough to keep you."

There was no point in lying. Rowan could easily cast any of a dozen spells to make me tell the truth. Since he was asking the question, he was waiting to see if I'd volunteer an honest answer on my own.

"I'm here because I'm your mate, and yes, I'm a Grand Mistress Necromancer as well. I went to see Mlinzi and Walinzi to ask them where to find the Sword of Theodora. They took all the Casters' memories of me in exchange for information on where to find the Sword." I met his intense gaze straight on. "I'm not your enemy."

Rowan tilted his head. "That didn't answer my questions about the wards."

"No, it didn't." I hated to share the truth here, as it made me even more vulnerable. I didn't see any choice, though. "Mlinzi and Walinzi took more than the Casters' memory as payment. I can't recall a single incantation." I shook my head. "I can pull in power, but not cast a spell."

Rowan stared at me for a long moment. "I don't believe you."

Those words shouldn't have hurt as much as they did. After all, Rowan couldn't help that his mind had been wiped of any memory of me. Still, there had to be a way to convince him. I tapped the ring on my finger. "See this? It used to be a mating band. Now it's a totem ring from Mlinzi and Walinzi. You have a matching one."

Rowan's gaze flicked to his hand. "I have a ring with an orange metallic sheen. Unlike yours, it has no carvings of monkeys on it. I fail to see how that proves anything."

I lifted my hand, palm forward. "Then touch me with intent. Your energy will flow into mine. That's mate power, and it doesn't require an incantation in order to work. Give me a chance and you'll see—we're true mates."

Rowan stared at my palm. The moment hung in its own little eternity. It took all my strength not to simply grasp his palm, but that's not how shared power worked. Rowan needed to want our magick to combine.

My hand began to tremble. "Please, Rowan."

Another long moment passed. Rowan's gaze locked with mine, and pure rage lit up his eyes. "I won't deny you're casting some kind of spell on me. My thoughts keep pulling me to you. It isn't right."

"It's the bond." My voice broke with grief.

"No, it's a spell. Another invention of Viktor's, no doubt. I wish I could interrogate you myself, but that won't be possible as long as I'm under this enchantment. But don't worry...Your master will not infiltrate my mind like he did so many of my senior Casters. I will not be led away from my people."

"I don't want that, Rowan. I'm here to help."

"What you *think* you want is of no consequence. I'm sending some of the palace mages to interrogate you, and they'll cast Thought Blade spells. You know how those work, don't you?"

"You wouldn't." Thought Blades were an excruciating way to die. You relived every agony of your life at once until both your mind and body fell apart.

"I won't. But my mages will soon enough." His voice lowered. "Even so, you won't be here when they arrive, will you? That story about not being able to remember incantations; I don't believe it for a second. Go on, escape. I'll find you and your master Viktor, no matter where you hide."

"No, please." My thoughts raced through everything I knew of Rowan. There must be some way to convince him. Sadly, I couldn't think of a thing. "Thought Blades are vicious castings. The palace mages will ruin my mind."

"Do you know what Viktor did to our families? Many of the Casters he lured away went insane, thanks to his experiments. The lucky ones died. You have no right to complain."

I scrubbed my hands over my face. "I know." When my hands dropped, Rowan had moved closer to me than ever before. If I went on tiptoe, I could brush my lips against his.

"And that's what makes you so dangerous, Necromancer. I believe that you do understand."

At those words, my heart cracked. In our quietest moments, Rowan told me how I was the only person to break through his lonely life as ruler, sharing his heart and burdens. Hope sparked in my soul. Perhaps some part of Rowan knew who I truly was. The weight of my mate's responsibility and loneliness seemed to age him before my eyes.

Suddenly, a flicker of movement happened in the periphery of the room, catching my interest. In the open window frame, two large green eyes were staring at me from outside the window. *Jicho.* The boy had somehow climbed up the outer rock wall and was waiting to come inside. He couldn't stay there for long before the guards spotted him, even if they had been sent away.

Rowan noticed my gaze shifting. "What are you looking at?" He started to turn around, and if he did, he'd see Jicho. No doubt, Rowan would put his younger brother under lock and key, and not let Jicho speak to me freely. Rowan had made that more than clear before when Jicho first approached me at the Caster festival.

I needed to distract Rowan and fast.

Moving quickly, I wrapped my arms around Rowan's neck and pulled him in for a delicate kiss. It was nothing more than a feather-soft touch, but I felt the warmth of Rowan's mouth through every part of my being. He stepped away from me as if I'd stuck him with a dagger.

"You…I can't…" Rowan shook his head and sped from the room. The moment the door slammed, I felt as if part of my life had been torn away. I'd pushed too hard to force that kiss. Now Rowan would see that as further validation that I really was some sort of spy from Viktor. Damn.

"Elea," whispered Jicho. "Help!"

I gasped. In my turmoil about Rowan, I'd forgotten all about Jicho hanging from the outside of the tower. I raced over to the open window, hoping that if I couldn't help Rowan, perhaps I could at least do something for his little brother.

After all, things weren't looking too bright for me. I knew Rowan. Right now, he was undoubtedly meeting with the palace mages, giving them instructions to do whatever they wanted, so long as they uncovered every secret in my head.

And those Thought Blade spells would indeed uncover my every memory. But they'd kill me in the process, and fast.

CHAPTER TEN

Rushing over to the window, I helped Jicho crawl into the room. The second his feet touched the floor, I ushered him to a spot against the wall.

"You need to stay out of sight," I warned.

Jicho brushed some bits of stone off his black Caster leathers. Normally, the boy wore Seer robes. He seemed to be up to something.

Something more than usual, that is.

Jicho lifted his chin. "I wouldn't have needed any help at all, but the rock out there is so old and weak. It's like crawling up a block of cheese." He set his fists on his hips, which was a movement I'd seen Rowan do a hundred times before. Jicho didn't want to show any weakness.

"You did very well, considering."

"Thank you. I climb everywhere around the castle. I'm really good at it, too." He gave me a gap-toothed smile. "I'm here to rescue you. That's why I'm wearing Caster leathers like Rowan."

My heart melted at that sweet-faced boy. "You look very dashing, Jicho." I knelt down so we could look each other in the eye.

"But you can't save me. I'll figure out something." I stepped back to the window and looked out. Sure enough, Kade's many soldiers were arrayed about the tower grounds. In the moonlight, I could make out a pair of figures in hooded red robes walking toward us. I'd seen that garb before.

Palace mages.

I stepped out of the window and spoke to Jicho again. "When the mages come, tell them I cast a spell on you to get you here. Then, you must leave."

Jicho's grin melted into a look of terror. "But the things they'll do to you, Elea. We can't let that happen."

I forced on my calmest Necromancer face. Inside, I wanted to scream and run. "You must leave, Jicho. I still need your help, and if the palace mages see you here, you know what Rowan will do. He'll lock you up in that Seer temple."

"No one is locking me up anywhere. Besides, I know where your friend Nan is. I've seen it. And I've had visions where we go and find her together."

My heart leapt into my throat. "But I can't cast anymore. We've no way to transport there."

Jicho lifted his chin. "I can lead you there."

"It's unsafe. You can tell me what you know, and I'll go and find Nan. My adventures tend to leave a trail of blood and bodies behind. It's no place for a nine-year-old boy."

Voices sounded under the tower window. The palace mages were chatting with the guard. We didn't have much time.

Jicho lifted his chin. "You can't argue with my visions. I've already told everyone that I'm meditating in the Seer temple for a few days. I do that sometimes after I've had a bad vision. Rowan always lets me. If I sneak off, he won't suspect a thing."

I frowned. "Rowan did say something about that at the festival. He gives you space when you've had a bad vision."

"That's right. Being spies runs in our blood. Plus, everyone will be so obsessed about the fact that you ran away, they won't care about me."

"But you're a—"

"I'm more than a kid, I'm a powerful Seer and the only one who understands what you're doing and can help you. You need me, Elea."

The bottom door to the tower opened with a long creak. I couldn't let Jicho see me get killed with a Thought Blade spell. The boy already had enough pain in his life.

"It's too dangerous, Jicho. Promise me you'll leave once the mages arrive."

"No, this is too important. I've had visions of Viktor, too. War is coming. We need that Sword. Nothing else will work." His large eyes glimmered with terror. "I've seen it over and again. Viktor will win, Elea. And he doesn't want to just rule. He plans to kill everyone."

My breath caught. "Are you sure?"

A tear rolled down Jicho's cheek, leaving behind a silver trail that glinted in the moonlight. "I'm positive." His lower lip wobbled. "And not just here. Other places, too. I saw this orange jungle get burned out...It's terrible, Elea."

Orange jungle. That was Mlinzi and Walinzi's world. Did Viktor's plan include them, too? My stomach soured at the thought. Destroying multiple worlds...I wouldn't doubt Viktor would do that and more.

I brushed the tear from Jicho's cheek. "All right. I accept your generous offer of help." I scanned the cell. "In that case, we now have to get out of here."

Jicho immediately brightened. It was just like a child to forget one terror with a new diversion. How I envied him that ability. "No problem," Jicho announced. "I can climb down and cause a diversion."

The footsteps in the corkscrew stairs grew louder.

"But I thought you were in meditation."

"Oh, yes." Jicho sighed. "Sorry. I didn't have a vision for how we'd get out of this. I only saw that we'd eventually escape."

I paced the floor, trying to force my mind to concentrate. Sure, I didn't have my magick, but wasn't Amelia always saying that magick was overrated? There had to be another way to escape.

With every step, the floorboards creaked ominously beneath my slippers. I froze midstep.

Suddenly, I knew exactly how we'd get out of this tower. I could only hope I had enough time left to enact my plan. Because unless I got past these mages and found the Sword of Theodora? There would be no stopping Viktor.

CHAPTER ELEVEN

Jicho and I simply had to escape this tower. In my opinion, the only way we could to do it was to pretend we'd already gone.

Fortunately, Rowan had trapped me in a tower that had been built more for storage than prisoners…And where things could be stored, they could also be hidden.

Falling onto my knees, I hooked my fingers around the edges of the nearest floorboard. It pulled up with ease. Sure enough, there was enough room in the sub floors for Jicho and I to hide, so long as we laid silently on our backs. Dust and old moldy oats lined the space. Someone had definitely used this for storage.

The footsteps in the tower staircase grew louder. The palace mages would be here any second. There wasn't time.

"We need to pull up the floorboards and hide underneath," I whispered to Jicho.

"Won't they know we're hiding?"

"Everyone thinks I can still cast magick. They'll assume I transported away."

"But what if they cast a tracking spell to find out where you went?" asked Jicho. "They'll know you're here."

"I don't think they will."

In truth, I figured that there was a good chance they would try to cast a tracker spell, but this was the best plan I could conjure with in all of three seconds. It wasn't the best plan in the universe, but it was better than standing around. And palace mages were often raised in comfort and luxury. They wouldn't know about storage spaces in towers.

Probably.

Hopefully.

Eh, this was insane.

Jicho slid out the floorboards and began to scoot under the subfloor. "Well, I won't hide and wait while they take you away."

"Agreed." I did the same as Jicho, pulling up enough boards so I could shimmy into the sub-floor. Lying on my back, I maneuvered the wood slats back where they'd been before. The moment the last board snicked into place, the door to the tower room slammed open.

A long pause followed. My heart thumped so hard in my chest, I thought it would be audible to the mages.

"She's not here," said an elder woman's voice. "Thank the Lady."

"We should cast a tracking spell." This time, it was a young man who spoke. I'd seen a pair of mages heading across the grounds. These must be the same two.

"No, we should not." The elder woman's voice deepened with conviction. I made a silent vow that if I got through this alive and retook my role in the palace, I was definitely awarding her property. By the Sire, she could have her own temple named in her honor.

"No, you heard Prince Kade's orders."

My teeth locked with frustration. The younger mage was most definitely not getting a temple.

"Yes, and I recall Genesis Rex saying that if we harm her, he'd want a full accounting."

My heart soared. I had heard Rowan's "*I want a full accounting*" speech many times. That was his way of telling the mages that he didn't want me harmed unnecessarily. Perhaps he was remembering more at last.

"That warning meant nothing," said the young mage.

The elder mage sniffed. "You ever seen a man defend his mate?"

"You can't believe that witch is truly the mate of our Genesis Rex."

"*That witch* told the king she was his mate. And she's a follower of Viktor, who is a master of enchantments. Who knows what kind of spells she's cast on our king? And if she can trick our Genesis Rex? She's a mage unlike anything we could fight. Rex would want us to go back. He's far better prepared to track and fight her than we are. If we go off and get ourselves killed, we're of no use to our king."

It was official. This woman would get two temples.

"I hadn't thought of it that way." The younger mage paced the floor. The movement of the boards sent bits of dust cascading into my mouth and nose. I stifled the urge to sneeze. Jicho didn't do as well. He let out a sound that sounded like a high-pitched squeak. My heart sank.

We'll be caught for sure.

"Did you hear something?" asked the young mage.

"It's an old room; it makes noises." The older woman's voice dripped with frustration. "Are we returning to the palace or not?"

Three temples.

"Fine," sighed the younger man. "We'll leave."

It seemed to take an eternity for them to march down the tower stairs. A low murmur of voices sounded from outside. I couldn't tell what they were saying, but I recognized Kade's voice in the mix. Next there came one of the most beautiful sounds I'd ever heard.

Three short whistles.

Kade was giving the code to retreat. They were all leaving the tower grounds. Jicho whispered to me from under the floorboards. "Should we get out Elea? This dust itches my nose."

"Not yet, Jicho. Let's give it a few minutes."

"This is the part I saw in my visions, Elea." Jicho's happy, sing-song voice carried under the floorboards. "Once they're gone, I'll lead us on our very own adventure."

Jicho was so excited I couldn't help but chuckle. "And how will you take me there?" No sooner did the question leave my mouth, than I knew the answer. "This is why you've been helping Amelia with the boat, isn't it? We're escaping on the river."

"Of course," said Jicho. "I've seen this coming for ages."

"I'm glad one of us did." Because if anyone had told me yesterday that I'd be hiding in the subfloor of one of Rowan's towers, I'd have said they were crazy.

Instead, it seemed like the world had gone mad.

CHAPTER TWELVE

After the palace mages left, Jicho and I waited under the floor-boards. Around me, thin shafts of moonlight broke through the wooden seams above my head. My thoughts kept returning to Rowan.

My miserable mate. When I last saw him, his green eyes had brimmed with pain. What a weight of loneliness he now seemed to carry.

I'll be back with you soon, my love.

After a while, the silence became deafening. Even the distant rumble of voices from the festival had died out.

"We can get up now," I said.

"That took forever," called Jicho.

Setting my hands flat against the boards above my head, I pushed until the wood flipped open. Standing up, I found my black Necromancer robes were now covered in a thin sheen of dust and dead bugs. I hadn't noticed the insects before. Thanks to my mage training, a single thought appeared in my mind.

Insect husks. What a nice source of death magick.

Then, I remembered that I couldn't cast any spells right now. The trickster gods Mlinzi and Walinzi had stolen every memory of an incantation.

Frustration tightened up my back. I was really starting to hate those two.

Leaning against the wall, I brushed the dirt off my robes, and contemplated my sorry state. How could I possibly find the Sword of Theodora without using magick? I straightened my stance and firmed up my determination.

Possible or not, there was no choice but to move forward.

I simply had to recall how to cast spells. A sigh escaped my lips. More importantly, Rowan needed to remember me. Soon. That left only one option.

Find Nan and the Sword.

I turned to Jicho. "I need to find my friend."

"Nan?"

"Yes. Nan has part of the Sword of Theodora. You said you had a vision of where she was?"

Jicho wiped at his face, which only served to make the dust at his cheeks turn darker. "I know where Nan is, and I'll take you to her."

I opened my mouth, ready to give another speech about how all my quests tend to turn rather bloody and disgusting. But we'd covered this before and Jicho was right. Viktor wiping out many worlds was reason enough to take some risks.

I gestured toward the door. "In that case, lead on."

"Yes, fair death maiden." Jicho puffed out his chest as he marched toward the door. He couldn't be prouder about helping me on a real adventure.

I could only hope he wouldn't one day regret it.

CHAPTER THIRTEEN

When Jicho and I stepped outside, the landscape was absolutely deserted. No more guards or mages lurked in the shadows. Even the partygoers had vanished. This was how Caster parties always went. Once the king left, everyone fell into a drunken stupor.

Perfect.

Jicho and I left the tower and snuck past the nearby village. With every step, we were careful to stay behind trees and in secluded alleys. In truth, there wasn't much to hide from. Most of the Casters were drunk, asleep, or both. Jicho indicated the path we should take with slight gestures. Beyond that, he refused to tell me where we were going.

Most likely, he thought that if I knew the destination, I'd still try to find Nan on my own.

And yes, he was probably right.

Soon Jicho and I were racing along the edge of one the tributaries that connected to the main river. Moonlight glinted off the still water. The village was now far behind us. Here only a few ferns and stubby trees lined the water's edge.

Still no sign of any people. Excellent.

After a short run, we reached a small construction by the riverside. The spot consisted of a stack of large wooden boxes on the shore. Beside them, a thin wooden plank jutted out over the dark water. And at the end of that thin walkway, there docked the strangest boat I had ever seen.

Not that I'd seen many water vessels, mind you, but I'd visited a few. Tristan, my one-time friend who'd turned out to be a godling, had told me he was a merchant. What he really was, I may never know. Even so, I'd visited Tristan's ship from time to time. It was a stocky, wooden affair that bristled with sails and ropes. The moment I'd stepped on board, I'd instantly felt seasick.

But this boat was a sleek metal creation that had been roughly modeled into the shape of a giant shark. Round portal windows lined the sides of the vessel. The main back fin was a tent-like area that hid a small round tower. I'd seen these canister-like objects before in Amelia's drawings.

"That's a steam engine," I said.

"Quite right," announced Jicho. "Welcome to the Marvelous and Amazing Jicho Extraordinaire. I call it *MAJE* for short."

"That's quite a name."

"Thank you." Jicho sprinted along the thin plank of wood and landed on the ship's top deck.

I followed him, my jaw agape. I stepped gingerly around the gleaming bronze deck. Now, if this thing had been created with magick, I'd have felt rather at home. In fact, I could imagine the exact spells I would select to fashion something similar, most likely with bat wings and whale bones. But the fact that this was made entirely from metal and without a single spell? This was a far more impressive creation.

Square metal doors lined up neatly below my feet. "The floor is covered in doors. What's below deck?"

"Oh, all sorts of things." Jicho stepped up to the canister-like object under the fin-tent. He began fiddling with dials and pulling on levers. "There are storage spaces and miniature engines. I'll have her going in a matter of minutes."

"Is there no other way to find Nan?"

"Not unless you can cast a transport spell?"

I stared at the innumerable levers, switches, and gears. They seemed to cover every open inch of space inside the boat. "How long before Rowan comes looking for you?"

And takes you away. Not that I added that part.

"One day, maybe two." Jicho tapped a small dial with his pointer finger. "I told him my last vision was so upsetting, I was going into meditation at the main temple of the Lady. No one bothers me there."

"I think that's being a bit hopeful. My guess is he'll start tracking us right away." Not that we'd know it. Rowan was an expert at staying hidden. I could only hope we'd find the first part of the Sword before he decided to strike. "How long have you known we'd be escaping this way?"

"Oh, it's like I told you. I've seen this for ages and ages." Jicho screwed his mouth up to one side. "That's why I asked Amelia to build the boat." The steam engine began to hiss and sputter as it came to life. "Have you seen her laboratory lately?"

"Yes, and the fact that it overflows with metal now makes perfect sense." I paced along the deck. Every upright surface seemed to be covered with a dial or lever. "I need to understand how to operate this thing."

"Oh, I can explain it to you." Jicho then launched into a lengthy description of how he helped Amelia find bolts for the hull. Bolts.

This wasn't helping.

I cleared my throat. "Sorry to interrupt but—"

"Don't you want to hear how we got the bolts into Amelia's lab?"

"Very soon. But is there a manual or something I could read while you explain things? That would be most helpful." *Or helpful at all, actually.*

Jicho rubbed his chin, leaving a fresh smear of grease in his wake. "All of Amelia's plans are in this case." He kicked at a small box that had been bolted to the deck. "Take a look."

"Thank you." After twisting a few of the metal knobs, I opened the airtight case. The shiny box was jammed full of random scraps of paper and plans. I sighed. This was Amelia, all right. The girl wrote everything down, but she was a true slob at heart. I pulled out a stack of papers from the top and sat down by the steam engine. The many dials gave off a soft glow that I could read by.

"Not much help, is it?" asked Jicho.

"I'll figure it out," I replied. "I had to decipher all sorts of ancient Necromancer texts in the Cloister library. This can't be worse." I scanned the top sheet. Amelia's handwriting was nearly unreadable. "I take it back. It's worse. Even so, I'll figure it out. How long do I have before we reach Nan?"

"Depends on the weather and the river," replied Jicho. "I've seen some different futures for us. We should reach her village by morning. Perhaps earlier."

"Assuming Rowan doesn't find us first." I settled in, resting my back against the side of the boat. "Have you had a vision of Rowan finding us?"

"No," said Jicho. "And that means there are too many ways things could happen. There are countless possibilities for our adventure here. I only see visions when there are one or two options for the future."

"Oh, that makes sense." I knew very little about Seer powers, and now was not the time for a more lengthy tutorial. Instead, I returned my attention to Amelia's papers while Jicho manned the MAJE. In the moonlight, I could see the trees grow thicker along the shoreline. The air became heavier with moisture.

We were heading deeper into the jungle.

I smoothed out the sheet before me. "It looks like Amelia did the design here."

"Whenever she got stumped, I saw what she needed to do next." Jicho flipped a lever and a strange hiss erupted from the control panel. "Whoops." He cranked a hand dial and the steam stopped. "Do you want me to tell you about every vision I had? I can explain once I'm done telling you about the bolts." He scrunched up his mouth again. "Although then, you definitely need to know the story about how we get the sheet metal."

"You know what? I'm fine. I'll read these sheets and you get the MAJE going."

Jicho frowned. "If you're sure."

"Positive."

"I get it." Jicho grinned. "I'll give you a minute before I finish my bolt story. This is a lot for you to take in, what with you being so old and all."

"Thank you, Jicho." *I think.*

With that, I began deciphering what had been built into this metal contraption. After all, without magick the MAJE might my only way to get the Sword of Theodora...And the answer about how to heal the gateways without requiring my own death.

Assuming the Sire and Lady would even allow that.

I couldn't ignore the truth. Even if I could find hybrid magick to heal the gateways, the gods might fight against me anyway. The Sire and Lady clearly didn't like me wielding hybrid magick.

Right now, all that stood between Viktor's war and my death were a Seer boy, a strange metal boat, and me, a mage who had forgotten how to cast a single spell.

In other words, things were not looking good.

CHAPTER FOURTEEN

An important thing to remember about jungles: when night falls, the wildlife doesn't actually sleep. It's just that a different group of creatures awaken, ready to eat you alive. Like what seemed to be happening right now.

As the night deepened, a new chorus of chittering bugs and cawing birds sounded from either side of the river. Heavy growth encroached all around. Gnarled bodies of trees overtook the shoreline, digging into the water with long finger-like roots. Vines and hanging moss cascaded from the tall tree branches. Soon, only a sliver of night sky was visible above us. The scent of old rot and fresh mud became stronger by the second. Worst of all, glowing yellow eyes stared out from the deep shadows.

It was beyond eerie. And since the morning had arrived, I now only had two days before the Martyr's Comet vanished. Not too helpful.

An odd screech broke through the morning air. On reflex, I gripped the sheet of Amelia's notes so tightly I almost tore the paper. Normally, I wouldn't be so jumpy. But then again, I usually had the ability to cast all the spells I wanted.

"What was that screeching noise?" I asked.

"Which one?"

"The sound that went—" Before I could finish, the creature in question screeched again. It sounded like a cross between an angry goat and a massive snake. The moment the cry was over, I pointed to the patch of jungle where the noise came from. "Just like that."

Jicho shrugged. "Eh, that's nothing to worry about. It's just a ruddy bird."

"Will it kill us?" Like every Caster, Jicho grew up in jungles. He had a deep memory of every creature and their function.

"Not while we're on the water. But if we get on land, it would scoop out our insides and wear our skin for camouflage."

"Understood." *Disgusting, but completely understood.*

"They don't sleep, either. Very strange. But they're tall and red, so they're pretty easy to avoid. Unless they're, you know, not."

"Got it. Tall red killer creature called a ruddy bird."

Now, I knew at some point that we'd need to get off this boat and talk to Nan. That didn't mean I was looking forward to that part of this adventure, though.

That said, there was one distinct benefit to travelling through the deep jungle with a Caster: the odd noises and staring eyes didn't bother Jicho at all. No matter what happened outside the MAJE, Jicho merely kept playing with the controls on his metal ship. For my part, I tried to act unaffected while I sat on deck, pouring over Amelia's handwritten notes. I couldn't have slept if I'd wanted to.

At least, the notes themselves were fascinating. Simply put, the things this boat could do were nothing less than phenomenal. Vast amounts of silk were stored inside the ship's hull, along with things that looked like massive ball bearings. Oh, and there were all sorts of knives and darts hidden within as well. How Amelia and Jicho got so much packed inside one vessel, I'll never know.

Not that I didn't try get answers from Jicho. That plan just hadn't worked out too well. Starting a conversation with the boy was troublesome at best. Every time I asked him a question, Jicho launched into a description of his beloved bolts while some kind of dial popped or whistle blew. Jicho assured me he knew exactly how to manage the *MAJE*—and that he could certainly chat while still keeping the boat afloat—but I had my doubts. All in all, things were just more silent and sane when both Jicho and I stayed focused on our respective tasks. Even so, it didn't stop Jicho from trying.

"Are you sure you don't want to hear about the bolts?" The moment the words left Jicho's lips, one of the dials let off a small geyser of steam.

I gestured at the errant dial. "I'm very clear on the bolts. Please focus on that steam. It looks rather dangerous."

"It's not." Jicho screwed his mouth up, which I was quickly learning meant that he wasn't quite sure how to fix whatever had gone wrong. "Let me tell you about the bolts. We sourced them from a tinker in the north lands. The fellow had a nose the side of a yam. Did I tell you about him?"

"Four times. How about we change the topic from bolts. What is the silk for, exactly?"

"All sorts of things." That was the best answer I could get from Jicho on critical items. "Oh, did I tell you that the tinker's name is Obadiah?"

"You did." *Six times.*

"Now this Obadiah—" Jicho paused, his gaze fixed on the water. All the color drained from the boy's face.

This wasn't good.

"What's wrong?"

Jicho didn't answer. Instead, he kept his gaze locked on a strange ripple on the water, as if something was moving under the river and heading toward us. I pointed to the spot. "Is that what you're looking at?"

"Yeah." All the color drained from Jicho's face. "I don't know what that is."

A chill crawled up my neck. "You don't?" Jicho was my resident expert on odd happenings in the jungle.

Jicho spun about in a slow circle. "There are more of them."

Standing up, I scanned the water around us. Sure enough, more of the strange waves were shifting across the surface of the river. About a half dozen *somethings* were moving toward us, their motions hidden by the dark river. My pulse sped.

The charge of magick filled the air, making my hair stand on end. An odd chill licked across my skin, followed by a strange heat.

Heat and cold.

Necromancer and Caster power.

I shook my head.

It couldn't be...

A pulse of violet light shot under the surface of the water.

It was.

Whatever was coming, it wielded hybrid magick.

My stomach twisted with worry and doubt. Yes, I couldn't cast any spells right now. But if I were about to face Caster or Necromancer magick, then I'd at least know what to expect.

Jicho moved to stand beside me. His small hand gripped mine. "You know what's coming, don't you?"

"Whatever it is, it's got hybrid magick."

"Then it's not your friend Nan?"

"Nan wasn't even a trained Necromancer," I explained. "She barely could pull in death magick, let alone hybrid." More waves of cold and warm energy moved across my skin. I shivered. "Whoever is casting this, they're as powerful as..." I stopped myself before saying *the Tsar Viktor*. Jicho was already wide-eyed and panting.

Suddenly, a bony arm burst through the water's surface, the skin covered in what looked like bubbling tar.

My eyes widened. I'd seen that tar-like effect once before when I'd spied on the Sire and Lady. Back then, the Sire's hand had glowed with hybrid power before he spoke the words that still haunted me: *"hybrid power always corrupts."* After that, the Sire's hands turned as black and bubbling as the ones before me now.

I didn't like that, not one whit.

The hand dug into the water's surface with claw-like fingers. Whatever this thing was, it treated the water as if it were solid instead of liquid. After that, a creature dragged itself out form under the surface of the water. It was tall and bony with an over-sized head. Every inch of its body seemed to bubble and sag with tar. All-yellow eyes peered at me from a massive face with droop-ing features.

It strode across the surface of the water, staying a few arms lengths from the side of the ship as it slowly lumbered along the surface of the water, keeping pace with the ship.

Jicho scooted behind me a bit, his grip on my hand tightening. Using my Necromancer training, I schooled my features into a semblance of serenity and confidence.

"Who are you?" I asked.

"We are the Rushwa." The creature's voice was a deep gurgle. "I am *the* Rushwa."

My brows lifted. "You are a we?"

The creature chuckled as six more creatures broke through the surface of the water. Like the first monster, these all hauled them-selves onto the water's surface and then walked over.

"We," repeated the Rushwa.

At that moment, the ruddy bird let out another ear-piercing squawk. The sound sent waves of movement through the Rushwa. The creature hissed in pain.

I pursed my lips. So loud noises affected the Rushwa. *Interesting.*

Jicho shook my wrist. "Look, Elea!"

Spinning around slowly, I scanned the waters nearby. Together, these seven monsters now surrounded our little vessel, stepping along in unison as they followed our journey along the river.

Now, I couldn't cast a spell, but the Rushwa didn't know this. Focusing my mage senses, I pulled in Necromancer power from around me. Bones lined the riverbed and lay embedded deep in the jungle floor. To me, they all seemed to vibrate with magickal echoes of their lives. I drew the power into my soul and focused it into my limbs. My forearms soon glowed blue with Necromancer power. I made sure to show them off as I spoke.

"If you value your existence, you'll go back where you came from. Leave us alone."

The Rushwa gave another gurgling laugh. It stepped around the MAJE until it reached the next Rushwa in line.. A short burst of violet light encircled the two Rushwa as they merged into one, larger entity.

I blinked hard, not believing what I was seeing. The creature didn't appear to be solid, but some kind of liquid lighter than water and just as malleable.

This was magick unlike anything I'd ever heard of before.

Jicho buried his face in my side. "What are those things, Elea?"

"Listen to me carefully. This deck is lined with doors. Do any of them lead somewhere you can stay safe?"

The merged creature stepped into the next Rushwa in line, getting larger.

Four creatures remained.

Jicho nodded. "Most of them are big enough to hide in."

"Good." I exhaled. "Then you need to go into one and stay put until I'm done here."

"You're going to fight them, aren't you?"

Only two left now.

"I'm going to try. That's why you need to get someplace safe."

"I'll try." Jicho's voice warbled with fear. "But I need to run the ship aground and turn off the stream engine."

"Do whatever you—"

Before I could finish my thought, a massive hand wrapped around my waist, hauling me off the MAJE's deck. Before I knew what was happening, the thing had jammed me into its mouth, swallowing me whole.

One moment, I was struggling against a monster's grip. The next, I was surrounded by oily slop, unable to breathe or see. Panic boiled through my bloodstream, but I was able to lean into

Necromancer training once more. With force of will, I kept my mind and body calm.

After that, I pulled even more Necromancer power into my body.

It was true that I couldn't cast a spell, but that didn't mean there was no benefit to pulling in power. Before I got trained as a Necromancer, I used magick to help with chores like chopping wood. Later on at the Cloister, I channeled the same power to climb the Zelle mountain. Petra said it helped my focus.

Petra. I pictured her once-beloved face tightening into a lined scowl. What would she say if I became this creature's meal instead of Tsarina? The answer came from the pit of my soul.

Petra would say nothing because the Rushwa are not going to kill me. I'm climbing out of this monster's stomach and then...

And then, I'd think of something.

Maybe.

Hopefully.

In reality, I had no plan here and very little chance of survival.

Even so, my lungs burned for air as I pushed all my magick into my forearms. After that, I scaled upwards. The creature's throat was slimy and bubbled with the same sick energy. My power thrummed through my hands as I blindly crawled higher. When I got to the monster's mouth, it let out a loud roar of frustration and pain. A welcome burst of air surrounded me. I took in a deep breath and held it in tightly.

That's when I remembered the ruddy bird. The Rushwa had shivered with pain when that animal screeched. A plan formed in my mind. I had a lung full of air and magick that could enhance anything physical that I did. What if I tried some screaming of my own?

It wasn't the best scheme, but it was better than nothing.

Using all my focus, I channeled my magick into my throat and voice box. My neck glowed with blue light as I set loose the mother of all screams. The gooey structure of the creature shivered around me.

After that, it burst apart.

I landed in the dark waters with a splash. Kicking my legs, I propelled myself through to the river's surface. Bits of oily goo floated around me.

Now, I'm a death mage, but even I found that disgusting.

The ship was aground, so I paddled over to the side of the boat and hauled myself onto the deck. If there was one consolation in this battle, it was that my quick post-fight swim served to wash off most of the black tar from being ingested by that hybrid monster.

The moment I set foot on deck, one of the small doors on the floor flipped open. Jicho popped his head out. "Did we win?"

He seemed so excited, I couldn't help but smile. "We did." I rubbed my forehead. "There's no time to celebrate, though. We need to get this ship back in the water and find Nan."

"Sure thing," said Jicho. "I have a toolkit that can help." He knelt down and pulled at one of the small doors set into the deck of the ship.

All of a sudden, an arrow whizzed an inch away from Jicho's nose, landing with a thunk on the metal deck.

Jicho hopped to his feet. "What was that?"

More arrows passed right by his skin, each one zinging close enough to scrape him without drawing blood. I'd seen this kind of attack before.

"Move slowly," I warned. "Someone is warning us."

Jicho rolled his eyes. "Uh, I think they're trying to kill us."

"Each of those arrows perfectly brushed you without striking. If they wanted to you injured, they would have done it by now. No, whoever it is, they want our attention."

I raised my hands to shoulder height and palms forward. Little by little, I rose to stand and turned about to face the jungle. "We won't attack you. Come out."

A moment later, the jungle was filled with yellow eyes. Thousands of them. And they were staring straight at me and Jicho. The last time we saw those particular kind of glowing eyes, they were attached to tar warriors who tried to kill us.

Not an encouraging thought.

Rustlings sounded from the depths of the jungle. The yellow eyes grew brighter and larger. *Whoever was out there, they were closing in.* I held my breath and thought through my options. There weren't many.

Straightening my spine, I prepared to meet whatever new menace approached.

CHAPTER FIFTEEN

Gripping the *MAJE*'s metal railing, I peered over the side of the vessel. The metal hull remained half-deep in mud. *Damn.* We were still run aground.

Jicho pulled on my sleeve. "Elea, the jungle."

Shifting my focus, I scanned the shoreline. A few yards away from the ship loomed a wall of hanging moss and heavy vines. Moonlight glinted off the emerald leaves.

That's when I saw it.

A pair of bright yellow eyes peered out from the darkened jungle. I'd seen that look before. *The Rushwa.* My heart pounded with such force, I could feel my pulse in my skull.

I just fought seven Rushwa. Surely, I can defeat one more.

Dozens more pairs of eyes then blinked into view. I quickly tallied up how many Rushwa I might be facing.

Ten...Twenty...A little over thirty.

A pang of worry tightened my throat. Seven Rushwa were hard enough. But more than thirty?

Little by little, a gangly figure stepped out from behind the vines. Based on the build, it was definitely a man, only one unlike any other I'd seen before. He wore a bone helmet with thick horns that jutted out and up on either side, reminding me of a water buffalo. The helm covered his face down to the nose, leaving only enough upper space for his luminous yellow eyes to peer out. The rest of the stranger's slim body was covered in thin gray fur. A round silver amulet hung from a cord about his neck.

Not the Rushwa, then. My shoulders slumped with relief. Whoever this was, perhaps he knew how to find Nan and the Sword.

I waved from the deck. "Greetings, I'm Elea." I wrapped my arm around Jicho's shoulders. "This is Jicho. Can you help us? We need someone to push our boat back into the river."

The man waved me closer. Leaning his head back, he let out a series of guttural growls accented by chirps. The sound was melodic and purposeful.

This was his language, only I couldn't interpret a word.

"Sorry, I don't understand."

The man let out more speech-like sounds. After that, he moved his arm in a circular motion toward his chest. The intent was clear: *come here.*

I knelt down to look Jicho in the eye. "I'm going to talk to him. Can you stay abroad the ship?"

Jicho spoke in a child's whisper, which was really no whisper at all. "Amelia and I planned some special things into the ship. I might be able to help." He scrunched up his face. "The *MAJE* is designed do amazing things, but…" Jicho kicked at the deck.

"But what?"

"We never could get any of them to work. The ship kept exploding."

My eyes widened. In this situation, the words *ship* and *exploding* were not good at all. "I have an idea. Why don't you stay aboard the *MAJE*? If anyone comes after you, then you can hide again."

Jicho rubbed his neck, his eyes lost in thought. "That's probably a good idea."

Probably? Try definitely.

"I'll return shortly." I gave Jicho's shoulder an awkward pat. Casters usually hug each other, but I was still getting used to all that. Necromancers considered the need for physical contact to be a sign of weakness.

Slipping over the side of the vessel, I landed in the mud with a splash. My Necromancer robes had gotten soaked in my battle with the Rushwa. Now I was sopped in mud up to my kneecaps.

How I wished I could cast a cleaning spell.

Hiking up my skirts, I slogged through the mud and stepped toward the strange man. As I got closer, I got a better look at his appearance. It turned out, the man wasn't actually wearing a helm; the horns were an extension of his brow bone and actually part of his face. Whoever he was, this man was definitely some kind of magickal hybrid of a human and a water buffalo.

I paused. Could this man be a Changed One? I scanned him carefully. No, that wasn't a fit. Changed Ones were typical humans with an animal body limb, such as a snake for an arm or the legs of a cheetah. This man was something else: a true combination of human and animal. Although, I'd seen that by transform into a lion hybrid, but he'd been wild with fury. This man was calm.

I shrugged. *Ah, well.* The realms were filled with all sorts of marvels we had yet to discover. I'd never seen anything like this man before, but that didn't mean his kind hadn't been living in the jungle for ages.

Glancing over my shoulder, I met Jicho's gaze. The question was in my eyes but unspoken, *Do you know who these people are?*

Jicho shook his head. The answer was clear. *No.*

The man let out another growl that was accented by deep trills. He waved his arm toward me again.

"I'm coming." I lumbered my way up the shoreline until I stood only an arm's length away. Now, I could see intricate patterns of runes carved into the bones that wound out from his forehead. These were in Necromancer writing, so I could read them easily.

Mrefu, Keeper of Kila Kitu.

"Your name is Mrefu?" I asked.

The man nodded. Good thing certain movements were universal.

I tapped my chest. "Elea."

Mrefu launched into a long speech, accented by more growls and yips. His yellow eyes stayed locked with mine. The urgency in his gaze was unmistakable. Whatever he was telling me, it was important that I understand.

"I'm sorry," I shrugged. "I don't know what you're saying."

Mrefu hunched over, dipping his arm into the muck. When he stood up again, he started talking once more, only this time he was pointing to his darkened arm.

I frowned. "Is there something wrong with the mud?"

Mrefu huffed in frustration. After that, he began picking up great handfuls of mud and slopping them onto the downward curl of his horns. At last, I made the connection.

"You're talking about the Rushwa."

Mrefu nodded. His voice deepened as he spoke in snarling tones. He then mimed biting at his arm. Now, I knew exactly what he was talking about.

"That's right. The Rushwa attacked me. They tried to consume me alive, but I defeated them."

Mrefu began gesturing to the forest. All of a sudden, the eyes didn't seem so much to glare as to stare at me in appreciation.

"The Rushwa were your enemy too?"

Mrefu pounded his chest with his fist. The growling became plaintive. He turned his palm to face me. His furry palm glowed with purple brightness. The words of the Sire and Lady reverberated through me. *"Hybrid magick always corrupts."*

I tilted my head, thinking. "You and your people wield hybrid magick."

Mrefu nodded.

An image of the Rushwa appeared in my mind. Those creatures were tall and lanky, just like Mrefu. The Rushwa also had oversized heads, but that could easily be an illusion caused by the tar-like corruption covering their horns.

"I think I understand now," I said. "You wield hybrid magick but some of you became corrupted. The Rushwa."

Mrefu nodded again.

"So I did you a favor when I killed them. And now, will you do me a favor in return?"

Mrefu spoke once more. This time, his voice took on a happy and almost musical air. With a graceful motion, he crossed his arms over his chest and bowed his head.

I grinned. "I'm going to interpret that as a yes."

Mrefu raised his head to meet my gaze. Determination shone in his eyes and he called out something in a loud voice.

In reply, a new voice echoed through the jungle. "Mrefu, don't you dare!"

The hair on my neck stood on end. That voice sounded familiar. *Was it Nan?*

"Draw your weapons. Now!"

Oh, that was Nan all right.

But how did she come to know Mrefu and his people? And why would she order them to threaten me?

In response Nan's cry, things happened so quickly that I barely saw the blur of motion erupting around me. One moment, I was asking Mrefu to confirm his name. The next second, a dozen figures had stepped out from the jungle. All of them looked like Mrefu, only their gray fur had a purple sheen. Unlike Mrefu, each one carried a bow and arrow. Unfortunately, their weapons were drawn and pointed at a single target.

My throat.

Every muscle in my body tightened. This was not a good development. Sure, I knew a little fighting. Rowan's brother Kade had taught me a nerve pinch that I could use on someone at close range. That said, I knew nothing about how to defeat so many without magick.

Jicho waved his arms. "Leave her alone! She's my brother's mate!"

I forced my manner into the perfect image of Necromancer serenity. "It's fine, Jicho. I have it under control."

In truth, I had no idea what would happen next. But my words seemed to calm Jicho, so there was that.

"Why don't you check on things below ship?" I asked. With so many drawn arrows, I wanted Jicho out of harm's way.

Jicho screwed his mouth up for a moment. "Oh, sure. Of course." His face brightened with a huge smile. "I'll stay below deck." He shot me an exaggerated wink. "There's plenty to do." The boy spoke in rapid-fire style, which meant that he was hatching some kind of plan.

"Jicho, just stay hidden and don't make anything—" Before I got the chance to say the word *explode*, Jicho had already disappeared below deck.

The moment Jicho was gone, Nan stepped out from behind the wall of green. She looked just as I remembered: a girl in her late teens with ebony dark skin and long braids. She wore a loose leather jerkin and cotton pants. I exhaled. My mind hadn't been playing tricks on me, after all.

Nan was really here. Huzzah!

Surely, she had mistaken me for someone else before. Once Nan realized I was her Elea, things would move forward quickly. I could almost imagine myself grasping the Sword of Theodora… Healing the gateways with ease…And doing it all before the Martyr's Comet disappeared from the sky.

As Nan stepped closer, Mrefu gave her an approving nod. My heart soared. The two of them were allies. That settled it. Nan would somehow intervene on my behalf. Although it wasn't very Necromancer-like of me to show such emotion, I couldn't help it. I grinned. "I can't believe you're alive!"

Nan merely stared at me, an unreadable look on her face. I decided to keep talking. Nan was a total chatterbox. If I spoke enough, she would definitely join in. For their part, the warriors kept their weapons aimed at my throat. I did my best to ignore them and press forward. It seemed that no one was giving them the order to shoot, which I took as a good sign.

"What happened to you?" I asked. "How did you come back from the dead?"

Even though I asked the question, I already knew one possible explanation. Recently, I'd raised thousands of Necromancers from the dead during a battle with Viktor. But all those mages had skull markings on their faces. I carefully inspected Nan's skin. Perfect ebony. It was almost too ideal, actually.

I worried my lower lip with my teeth. Perhaps someone else had raised her from the dead, removing any imperfections along the way. That wasn't an easy spell to cast—and there were few Necromancers left around who could even attempt it—but the magick certainly wasn't impossible.

Nan raised her arm. "Shoot!"

I still had some magick left in my body after the battle with the Rushwa. I now focused that power into my arms, ready to deflect any arrows.

Leaping to stand, Mrefu stood before me, blocking the attack. With a series of roars, he out a set of counter-orders. The warriors didn't release an arrow.

Mrefu was my new favorite person.

Still ignoring me, Nan rounded Mrefu. "You heard my order. They must shoot this intruder."

I returned my focus to Nan. When I spoke again, I hated the quiver that had crept into my tone. "Please. You are my friend, aren't you?"

Nan kept her gaze locked with Mrefu. "I saved your life from the Rushwa. You owe me. Do it. Order them to kill her."

Mrefu let out a low growl; Nan replied with a similar set of noises. I had the sinking feeling they were discussing whether or not to skewer me. Did I think that things were not going well before? The situation had just gotten a lot worse.

"Nan, it's me. Elea. Don't you recognize me?"

"I know who you are," said Nan slowly. "You're a spy for Viktor and Petra."

My eyes widened with surprise. "You're wrong. I came here because I need to find the Sword of Theodora so I can *kill* Viktor when he attacks. I was told you knew where this weapon was hidden, or at least where I could find part of it."

Nan tilted her head. "So, you're against Viktor."

"Of course. Viktor is raising an army. We must stop him."

"And what about Petra?"

Even hearing the name of my old Mother Superior made me flinch. "Petra and I are enemies now. She wanted me to rule the Necromancers. I refused."

Nan stared at me for a long minute. "I don't believe you. Petra tried to force me to learn Necromancy."

"Yet you didn't want to learn." Nan always had some raw Necromancer power, but zero desire to develop it.

"How can you say that? Of course, I didn't want to learn. Who wants to be a death mage? And because I refused, *you* ordered Petra to murder me."

"That never happened. I didn't rule the Necromancers. Never have. I'm not your Tsarina." I set my hand on my throat. "And if I did accept the throne, they'd kill me. In fact, they have a plan to end my life when the Martyr's Comet vanishes."

"Like I'd believe that." Nan folded her arms over her chest. "Petra cast spells. She showed me that she was only acting on your orders. You're the secret Tsarina of our people and you ordered me dead." She turned to Mrefu once more. "Kill her."

All the air sped from my lungs. It was as if someone had punched me in the stomach. Nan was my friend—we'd been imprisoned together at the Midnight Cloister. I'd never have survived without Nan's sharp mind and sunny outlook. And now she wanted me dead?

"You can't mean that," I blurted.

However, Nan wasn't paying any attention to me. Instead, she was locked in a growling match with Mrefu. I thought back to my encounter with Mlinzi and Walinzi. They'd talked about Nan and *the exiles*. Had she been banished out here with other Necromancers and then somehow became allied with Mrefu and his people? That would explain how she spoke their language and had a blazing hatred of Petra.

Nan let out a louder growl than usual, and Mrefu quieted. At last, she returned her attention on me.

Pure rage gleamed in her eyes. "I'll be kind, which is more than you did for me." She turned to the warriors. "Mrefu is right. While I rescued you from the Rushwa, Elea murdered the last of their kind."

The warriors all lowered their weapons. Hope sparked in my chest. Maybe I could turn this around after all.

I took a half-step closer to Nan. "I appreciate your kindness."

Nan flashed me her palm. "Go from this place. And when you see Petra, give her new orders. Tell her to leave us alone. Mrefu and the Zaidi have enough to do without fighting all your assassins."

"Petra is not my ally. If she's sending people here to kill you, I've had no hand in it. It's the truth, Nan. I'm not Tsarina."

"So leave anyway."

"I can't. Not without the Sword."

Nan eyed me for a long moment. "I still don't believe you. Petra warned us that eventually, you'd come to kill us." She gestured toward my left hand. "How long before you cast a spell and murder us all? The Zaidi help us, they don't deserve to be brought into our mage squabbles."

"If I wanted you dead, I'd have cast already." It was a lie, but it was the best I could do.

Nan sighed. "I'm part of a group of exiles now. This isn't just about my life. I have responsibilities to the other exiles and to the Zaidi."

"And I have responsibilities to every soul in our world. Please. Jicho and I came a long way to talk to you. I need the Sword of Theodora to fight Viktor. That's the entire truth. If you've any trained Necromancers in your group, they can even cast an honesty spell on me."

Nan narrowed her eyes. "We all refuse to get trained in that dark magick. That's our problem. Petra must have told you."

"Petra has told me nothing. And whatever she told you about me? Lies. In fact, the woman tried to lock me up and force me to rule."

"She tried to lock *you* up?" With that question, some of the tension seeped out of the air. A wisp of a smile curled Nan's mouth.

"She tried," I answered. "It didn't work for long." I answered her grin with one of my own. The weight of worry on my shoulders seemed to melt away a little bit. This was good. Nan and I were sharing smiles. That had to mean something.

Mrefu let out more growls. Nan listened and nodded. This time, I felt certain that things were going in a better direction. "Mrefu says there is one in his tribe who is strong with hybrid magick. Kila Kitu. He'll determine if you're worthy to live."

The connections formed quickly. First, there was the bubbling tar-like skin of the Rushwa. After that, I pictured Mrefu's hybrid magick. Finally, I remembered the words of the Sire and lady once more. *"Hybrid power always corrupts."*

Words tumbled from my mouth without my meaning to speak. "Do all the Zaidi wield hybrid magick?"

Nan shrugged. "To some extent. They don't use it often, though."

"Why? Is it because it turns them into corrupted monsters, like the Rushwa?"

"They don't cast spells like you do. They merely use the power to enhance what they do anyway, like using the bows and arrows."

"So they can't get corrupted because they don't cast spells."

"It's not that. Becoming corrupted has to do with intention, not the magick itself. If you use it for evil, it corrupts." Nan's features gentled. "I'm guessing you're nervous about meeting Kila Kitu, don't. He's been in control over his power ever since it was gifted to him two thousand years ago."

Despite the jungle heat, my blood chilled over. "And who was that?"

"You don't know?"

When I spoke, my voice was a hoarse croak. "Was it another Tsarina named Elea?"

Nan nodded slowly. "She came to these lands two thousand years ago, at the time of the last Martyr's Comet. Before she made her sacrifice, the Tsarina created the Zaidi."

"She taught them Necromancer runes."

"The runes are from the Zaidi." Nan chuckled. "It was the Zaidi who taught their language to *your* people." Nan stepped closer and gripped my upper arm. "You really don't know any of this?"

"I'm learning and for the record, I've no plans to be a sacrifice."

"Don't you won't be Tsarina?"

"So I can die to heal some gateways? No thank you. There has to be another way. I think I can use hybrid magick to accomplish the same goals. Would the Rushwa know anything about it? Any kind of hybrid spell could help."

"No, as I said, they don't cast like you do. But if you really want to avoid the prophecy of the Martyr's Comet, then you should hide. If you don't sacrifice yourself before the end of the Blood Comet, then they'll take someone else. And there's another super-power Necromancer out there. Until you take the reins of power, the job of dying is technically his."

"You mean Viktor."

"The man is evil and deserves murder anyway."

"I've looked into it, believe me. But that would mean setting Viktor loose from the realm where we imprisoned him, getting the Sword, and killing him at the right moment...Assuming he attacks first, since I won't kill in cold blood."

Nan smacked her lips. "I can see that plan has limits."

"Also, Viktor is in league with the Sire and Lady. They all want me to be the sacrifice."

Nan scrubbed her hands over her face. "That settles it. You cannot stay here, and you must *never* get your hands on the Sword of Theodora. It's for your own protection, Elea. That Sword is hidden for a reason. You simply must go. Maybe catch a gateway to another world."

Mrefu replied with another low grunt.

"Really?" Nan lifted her brows. "You still think we should take her to *Kila Kitu?*"

Mrefu nodded.

I rested my hand atop Nan's grip. "Please. Take me to Kila Kitu. Can he show me where to find part of the Sword?"

"If he decides that you're worthy, then he'll give you the Sword's hilt."

I scanned the night sky. The Martyr's Comet was starting its slow arc toward the horizon once more. I had perhaps a day and a half left. "If I find the Sword, I'll know how to heal the gateways. Let's go."

"You don't understand. Kila Kitu is a mage like no other. It won't be pleasant." Nan lowered her voice to a plaintive tone. "Just leave and hide."

"No. Take me to Kila Kitu, only..." I gestured toward the MAJE. "I want Jicho to go with me." It wasn't a great idea to take a young boy to see a strange mage, but leaving him alone in the jungle wasn't ideal, either.

Mrefu grunted again and Nan translated. "Mrefu says that the boy must not join us. Kila Kitu won't like it." She tilted her head, sending her long braids swinging. "Mrefu's role in the community is to act as liaison to Kila Kitu. If Mrefu says to leave the boy behind, then it's for the best."

I sighed. "I don't like the idea of leaving Jicho alone."

"The Zaidi will keep the boy safe." Nan straightened her stance. "You can cast a truth spell on me, if you like."

That settled it. If Nan was willing to subject herself to a spell, then I felt confident Jicho would be fine. "A truth spell won't be necessary. I trust you."

"Good." Nan scanned the river. "We must move quickly. We need to return before anyone else arrives."

The muscles of my back tightened with worry. "Who else is coming?"

"Someone." Nan shrugged again. "We don't know who is on your trail, though. They're rather stealthy."

Stealthy in the jungle? No doubt, Rowan and his Caster army were behind us. Not that I would share that theory with Nan. It had been hard enough to get her to take me to Kila Kitu. I didn't need any distractions.

That said, my list of worries was growing quickly. Right now, I had a mysterious new mage to confront, a missing Sword to find, a Caster army to worry about, and my own neck to save. And I'd only get the Sword hilt if this Kila Kitu said I was worthy.

Whatever that meant.

"Follow us," said Nan.

I cast a longing glance at the *MAJE*. Normally, I'd chat with Jicho before leaving. He was definitely hatching a plan when he scurried below deck. Sadly, there wasn't time for any discussion right now. I needed to follow a hybrid man and my ex-friend deep into the jungle in order to meet a mysterious mage. And just to prove how risky my life had become, I thought this was a positive shift in my circumstances.

CHAPTER SIXTEEN

Leaving Jicho and the *MAJE* behind, I followed Mrefu and Nan past the dozen or so Zaidi who were standing outside the jungle proper. After that, the three of us stepped past the sheet of vines that marked the border into the deeper jungle. Once inside, it took a moment for my eyes to adjust to the lower light. Only a few beams of silver brightness cut through the heavy cover of trees, casting odd shadows on the muddy ground.

There were Zaidi everywhere.

If I'd been surprised to see Mrefu, I was outright shocked to discover that there were literally hundreds of his people waiting nearby. I spied men and women, tall and short, and all of them covered in varying shades of gray fur with heavy forms atop their heads. Every last one of them stared at me as I walked past.

Mrefu, Nan, and I soon passed the larger group of Zaidi. Around us, the jungle trees grew heavier with fern-like leaves. Within a few minutes, we reached a small clearing that centered around a raised stone disc. At one point, this circular rock had once been covered in Necromancer runes, but that pattern had long ago been worn away.

Crouching down, Mrefu gripped the huge disc and shoved it aside to reveal a stone walkway that led underground. He lifted his chin and made another growling sound.

"He wants us to get in," said Nan.

"All right." It was an effort to keep appearing calm. Stepping into an underground lair wasn't exactly a smart endeavor.

With the massive rock moved away, a set of stone stairs was now clearly visible. The rough-hewn steps led directly into the jungle floor. I marched down them with Nan close behind. Once we were both inside, Mrefu hauled the massive stone slid closed.

It took another act of supreme focus not to yelp as darkness enveloped me.

Suddenly, Mrefu's yellow eyes lit up more brightly than ever before. Thanks to that extra light, I could now make out the rough contours of space we had entered. We were standing in some kind of stone passageway that led off in a single direction. Condensation, moss, and black vines covered the rock walls. My feet were chilled in ankle-deep water.

Without any announcement, Mrefu marched off into the inky blackness. His eyes cast twin orbs of yellow light before us. Nan and I followed. The three of us walked down for a bit before the passage opened up into a great hall.

And what a space it was.

The chamber was round and incredibly tall with a small circular platform in the center. The walls here were covered in the same mixture of moss and dark vines as the outer hallway. Torches were set into the walls, casting the room in flickering light. The air was so still and quiet, my every breath felt deafeningly loud.

Mrefu let out another growl, and the sound echoed in odd ways around the tall and circular space.

"He wants us to follow him to the platform," said Nan.

I opened my mouth, ready to ask where this Kila Kitu was, but I was able to stop myself first. Honestly, there was no point in posing the question. If there was one thing I'd learned about mages of all kinds, it was that they liked to make a big show about their entrances and exits. In fact, the ability to jump in out of nowhere was one of Jicho's favorite pastimes.

The three of us stepped up to the round platform in the center of the room. As we crossed the stone floor, every step caused another slosh through the ankle-deep water. The hairs on the back of my neck stood on end.

Someone was watching us.

I scanned the round room. The ceiling stayed hidden in darkness, so it was possible that people could be waiting up there. In truth, a small army could be hiding in that space. My skin prickled with awareness. Tiny sounds echoed in from the cavernous ceiling. I shivered.

Was someone lurking in the darkness above our heads?

I shook my head. *Don't think yourself into a tizzy, Elea.* You're in an underground lair with an incredibly powerful mage. No one is hiding above your head.

Closing my eyes, I practiced one of my old meditations for calm. By the time I'd reached the round platform, I felt in control once again.

Mrefu stood at the platform's edge. Nan and I followed suit. After that, Mrefu raised his arms and began a series of low growls. The sounds repeated, his voice rising every time. Now, I couldn't remember any words to a spell, but I still knew the rules of how to cast them. And what Mrefu was doing? It was the classic format for an incantation of summoning.

The realization sent a pang of grief through my soul. How I wished I could cast again, myself.

A puff of wind spun around the circular platform, setting my Necromancer robes slapping against my legs. The breeze soon picked up, carrying along larger bits of moss and black vine. Within seconds, the wind had grown into a small vortex that was whipping around the center of the stone disc. The rough outlines of a figure appeared within the column of air. No question who this was.

Kila Kitu.

When the gusts stopped, a Zaidi man stood at the platform's center. Just like Mrefu, his face was shaped with bone and horn. Only unlike Mrefu, this figure was actually made completely from moss and black leaves.

Not a living person, then. I'd learned of this in the Cloister. Some people gained such incredible levels of magick while alive, that once they died, they could still take a physical form. Sometimes their spirit-selves possessed humans or, in this case, they took a shape made from leaves, bark, and moss.

I straightened my back and spoke in my calmest voice. "Greetings, Kila Kitu."

"Well met, Elea of Braddock." The mage's voice was a deep and gentle whisper.

"You speak." I hadn't meant to say that aloud, but after Mrefu's unintelligible language, I'd expected the same from Kila Kitu.

"I do whatever is required." The mage grinned, showing off a mouth of impossibly sharp teeth. I shivered. Those definitely weren't made of moss. And there was a malevolent spark in Kila Kitu's eyes that set my nerves on edge. I'd already been toyed with by Mlinzi and Walinzi, and this mage had the same dark glee in his soul.

In other words, the quicker all this was over with, the better.

"If you know that I'm Elea of Braddock, then you must also be aware of why I'm here. I need the hilt of the Sword of Theodora. I also need to know how to heal the gateways with hybrid magick. Your magick has violet light. It's hybrid, isn't it?"

"That's right."

"Then, how do I cast a hybrid spell to heal the gateways?"

"That will be evident once you find the Sword of Theodora."

My shoulders slumped. "So I've been told."

By trickster gods. Which isn't comforting.

"And I may give you the Sword hilt," said Kila Kitu. "But only after I determine if you are worthy. Are you strong enough to know the truth?" Kila Kitu's voice became so melodious it was almost a song. I wasn't sure what to make of him. Friend? Enemy?

I lifted my chin. It didn't matter what Kila Kitu was. He had answers. "Yes, I'm strong enough. How can I prove that to you?"

"Give me your wrist. Then, you can see the past through my magick, so long as your blood flows." Kila Kitu bared his teeth, and again, I couldn't miss how the mage had a mouthful of glistening fangs.

On reflex, I turned to Nan. My onetime friend stared at me with her right brow arched. I remembered that face. It was her way of wondering if I had the mettle to go through with this thing. My focus moved onto Mrefu. He gave me the barest of nods.

Go on, Mrefu seemed to be saying. *This is the way.*

I crossed the raised platform to stand beside Kila Kitu. Little by little, I lifted my arm, holding it out toward the mysterious Seer. Kila Kitu's moss-dark eyes glared at me. His mouth opened wide. The invitation was clear.

Set your hand in here.

I took one step closer.

Two.

Three.

Fast as a heartbeat, Kila Kitu latched his teeth into my wrist. A blast of hurt shot up my arm. Blood dripped from my skin, landing on the platform with a pit-pat. I gasped with shock.

The next thing I knew, the stone room disappeared. The pain vanished as well. The surprise I'd felt before morphed into curiosity. What spell had Kila Kitu cast? Purple smoke surrounded me, cutting off my vision. A charge of magick filled the air, reminding me of the promise of lightning before a storm.

Kila Kitu was casting a spell and without using an incantation. *Now that was powerful magick indeed.*

The violet mists faded away, revealing the fact that I no longer stood in the underground chamber of stone. Now, I waited at the edge of a great field whose grass was formed into red and blue squares. The pattern reminded me of the chess games I used to play with Petra back at the Zelle Cloister. Lining the edges of the field were gateways. Some were made of gemstones; others were simple gray bricks. I recognized the one I'd passed through to see

Mlinzi and Walinzi. All of them were empty arches whose hollow insides looked out over the vast checkerboard fields. I was the sole figure to be seen.

I looked down at myself for the first time. My body was a translucent as a ghost, while my right hand was torn up at the wrist. Blood dripped onto the earth, leaving no stain behind.

Clearly, I was a lone pawn in this game of gods and gateways. I didn't like that at all.

A ghostly version of Kila Kitu appeared beside me. Unlike back at the stone chamber, he looked like the rest of the Zaidi, only his fur was pure white. "You've made it through my casting. I'm impressed."

"What is this place?"

"This is the Meadow of Many Gateways. From here, we're connected to every world that contains life."

I scanned the landscape. Around me stood gateways of many different shapes and sizes with one thing in common: they all glowed with bright purple light. Another realization appeared. "Hybrid magick created this place. It's the power that connects everything together."

Kila Kitu tilted his head. "Somewhat."

Implications whirled through my mind. "Then it really is true. Our world is some kind of hub to control all the passages between realms."

Kila Kitu stared up into the night sky. "The Sire and Lady created the gateways. Every two thousand years, another Elea and Viktor are born, their bodies brimming with Necromancer power. The Sire and Lady believe they must recharge the gateways."

"So the Sire and Lady can control all the worlds."

"Yes. Even so, others believe the Martyr's Comet has a different purpose. They believe that the comet gives you extra magick not to power the gateways."

"Mlinzi and Walinzi told me about this. They want me to ensure they are freed from the gateways."

"There is more at stake than the tricksters. You might have the power to free all the captive worlds."

For a long moment, I could only stare at Kila Kitu, open mouthed. Once I found my voice again, I couldn't stop the words from tumbling out. "So this is more than merely saving my own world, but freeing all of them? This is too much."

Kila Kitu sighed. "You don't have a heart like my Elea. She would have leapt at the chance to help others. Perhaps we should return."

"Wait. This is a representation of the past. The gateways here were just powered with the energy of another Elea and Viktor."

"Yes, what you see here? The sacrifice was just made by my Elea. She created my people, the Zaidi. She gifted me with extra power."

"Take me back further in time. Show me how she died."

Pain glistened in Kila Kitu's eyes. "I won't do that."

"Then show me how the gateways were created."

Kila Kitu sniffed. "I *can't* do that. I'm not powerful enough."

"Then show me what you can. If I see how she died, there might be a clue about how to save all the gateways. I do want to save them. I'm just different from your Elea. A little more cautious, that's all."

"I will take you back. Then we'll see what you truly are." Kila Kitu waved his arm and a cloud of purple smoke appeared around us. A moment later, the violet-colored mists disappeared.

Kila Kitu and I still stood on the Meadow of Many Gateways. However, this time all the arches only shone with only the palest purple light. They were almost out of magickal energy.

Soon, someone would need to recharge them by losing their life.

The thought made me nauseous, but I leaned into my Necromancer training and kept my focus on the gateways. I simply had to stay alert. Seeing this so-called sacrifice might help me figure out how to power the gateways without losing my life.

I scanned the skies once more. The last of the Blood Comet was disappearing by the horizon.

Behind us, a gateway flared with a pale lavender light. Out of it stepped two figures I'd seen before in my visions.

First, there was an Elea who wasn't me.

And at her side, there walked a Viktor who wasn't Viktor.

The two were dressed in long purple robes that flowed behind them as they crossed the checkerboard grass. About twenty Zaidi followed behind them, all warriors who were carrying bows and arrows. The entire company marched right through both me and Kila Kitu, oblivious to our presence.

Kila Kitu gestured toward the Not-Elea and Not-Viktor. "You asked to see this. Why not have a closer look?"

What I wanted to do was run home and hide, but I nodded instead. With hesitant steps, I approached the Not-Elea. Her eyes were smaller than mine, her mouth a bit larger, and her nose a tad longer. She wasn't me, and yet she was.

After that, I looked to Viktor. It was the same with him; there were a series of subtle differences that added up to a single conclusion. This wasn't the same man I'd fought so many times before. The pair paused in the center of the long rectangular board. Viktor patted Elea's head and smiled.

They were friends.

I stared at them, my mind blank with shock. They liked each other? I'd assumed the two were mortal enemies, the same as me and my Viktor. Something about their friendship knocked at the back of my mind—this was important. I pictured my last battle with Viktor, the one where I raised the Necromancers from the dead. He'd cut his cheek and the same injury appeared on me.

And this Elea and Viktor were friends.

Together with the joint injuries, that meant something.

Before I could contemplate further, another gateway flared to life. Two new figures stepped onto the chessboard.

The Sire and Lady.

The Lady appeared resplendent as ever in her long green gown with golden tresses trailing behind her. For his part, the Sire wore his black armor and a dour look on his pale face. As the two approached the Not-Elea and Not-Viktor, the ground shook. Long fissures opened up in the checkerboard pattern of the meadow.

The Sire and Lady paused before the Not-Elea and Not-Viktor. The Lady gestured to the fresh breaks in the earth. "We don't have much time."

Not-Elea straightened the lines of her long purple robes. "I can access hybrid magick."

The Sire's gray eyes narrowed to slits. "Hybrid power is forbidden."

Not-Viktor gestured around the meadow. "But you created these gateways with hybrid power. Surely, we don't have to die to maintain it."

"Only one of you has to die," said the Lady. "But if you both choose to make the sacrifice, the arches will be that much stronger."

Another gateway lit up with purple brightness. This time, a figure in long bronze robes stepped out. Whoever it was, they were carrying the Sword of Theodora by the hilt, the blade pointed down. The robe's hood hung low, so I couldn't see the newcomer's face. Still, there was something solid and unyielding in their stance.

"Your executioner is here," said the Lady.

My throat constricted with anxiety. No wonder this figure appeared so foreboding. One day, whoever this was would come for me as well.

"Make this easy on yourself," added the Sire, his voice deep as thunder. "Sacrifice willingly. That way, it won't hurt so badly. For you…" He gestured to the Zaidi. "Or for them."

Not-Elea's shoulders stiffened. "You wouldn't hurt the Zaidi." Behind her, all the warriors strung their bows, pointing the arrows straight at the Sire and Lady. Neither of the deities so much as flinched with worry.

"We never hurt anyone," explained the Lady. "The executioner does."

Not-Viktor gripped Not-Elea's shoulder. "I know what you're thinking. Do not do this."

Not-Elea shook off his touch. "If I agree to this sacrifice, will you allow the Zaidi to live?"

The Lady smiled sweetly. "You have our word."

Not-Elea nodded and then knelt before her executioner.

After that, things happened so quickly, it was hard to keep track. Not-Viktor lunged for the executioner, ready to attack. The figure in bronze moved with supernatural speed, running the Sword of Theodora straight through Not-Viktor's chest. A burst of purple light shone out from the spot. Not-Viktor screamed in agony.

"See?" asked the Sire. "When you're unwilling, it's far more painful."

For a full minute, cries of agony echoed across the meadow. Then Not-Viktor fell over, dead.

Next the executioner turned to Not-Elea. My almost-double stared at the dead body beside her on the ground. "Say it again. You won't touch the Zaidi. You won't harm anyone else I love."

I gasped with recognition and fear. Those words reminded me of Petra's message. *"When you disobey the gods, this is what happens to those you love."*

How many times had the Sire and Lady blackmailed someone like me into allowing themselves to be killed? A ball of rage tightened inside me.

"We give you our word," intoned the Sire.

Not-Elea bowed her head. "Then I am ready."

One of the Zaidi stepped forward. "You cannot do this." My eyes widened as a recognized this young warrior.

It was a younger version of Kila Kitu.

Not-Elea gave him a sad smile. "You can't stop this. No one can. And I need you alive. Help the next martyr, so long as he or she is worthy."

The young Kila Kitu shook his head. "I can't."

"I am your creator. You owe me your life and fealty." The words Not-Elea spoke were harsh, but there was no anger behind them.

The young Kila Kitu hung his head. "I will do as you command."

"Move on with the ceremony," said the Lady.

"Wait," said Not-Elea. "I want all the Zaidi safely away first."

Grumbling sounded from the small company of warriors, but the Sire spoke in such a thunderous voice, they quickly silenced. "The sacrifice is correct. You may go." The Sire pointed to a nearby gateway, which flared with pale purple light. One by one, the Zaidi marched off the Meadow of Many Gateways. The younger version of Kila Kitu was last in line.

When the last of the Zaidi were gone, the executioner raised the Sword of Theodora. The blade seemed to move in agonizingly slow motion as it was brought down on Not-Elea's neck. Another flash of purple light appeared, just as when not-Viktor was killed, only brighter. Not-Elea instantly fell over, dead. There were no marks on her body. She hadn't even gasped, let alone screamed.

Somehow, that felt worse than how Not-Viktor died. At least, that was a real murder with agony and magick. This painless death seemed to mask the loss.

Beside me, Kila Kitu stirred. "I must end the vision now." His voice shook with emotion.

He'd loved his Elea.

"Please," I said. "I know this is hard for you, but I must see how the gateways take in magick."

Kila Kitu nodded. In the scene before us, a gateway flared to life once more. The younger Kila Kitu rushed back out from the arch, his body bright with purple light and hybrid magick.

The younger Kila Kitu raced toward the executioner, his speed enhanced by magick. Quick as a whip, the young Kila Kitu grabbed for the Sword of Theodora. At the same time, a cloud of purple mist enveloped them both. I'd seen that particular kind of swirling haze before. The younger Kila Kitu was casting a transport spell.

When the haze cleared away, the executioner was left standing alone on the meadow. The younger Kila Kitu had transported away. I stepped in for a closer look. Sure enough, the executioner now held only the blade of the Sword of Theodora.

I turned to the present-day version of Kila Kitu. "You only took the Sword's hilt. Is that because the executioner kept the blade?" Such things often happened with transport spells. If one part of an object was outside the sphere of the spell, it would get left behind. When it was a thing that got split into pieces, that wasn't so terrible. It was only when human beings tried to join a transport in progress that things got truly ugly.

"Yes, I was able to leave with the hilt. And my having it is what brought you to me."

"And now you wish to keep your promise to your Elea." I looked down at the ghostly version of my body. More blood dripped from my fingertips. Spots appeared in my vision. "And will you help me?"

"I do not yet know if you are worthy," answered Kila Kitu.

My back teeth locked with frustration. Why didn't Kila Kitu simply give me the hilt? Still, he hadn't said he wouldn't do so, only that he was unsure. There was still time to convince him, and I could be rather compelling when necessary.

In the scene before us, the Sire lifted the body of Not-Viktor. Meanwhile, the Lady did the same with Not-Elea. After that, the deities carried their burdens toward the nearest gateway. All the while, the executioner watched on silently.

My chest constricted, making it hard to breathe. The vision before me seemed too terrible to be real. Not-Elea and Not-Viktor were dead. This was like witnessing my own death.

The Sire and Lady set the lifeless bodies onto the thresholds of two nearby gateways. Instantly, the corpses of Not-Elea and Not-Viktor seemed to come to life once more. The pair convulsed on the threshold, their eyes wild and unseeing. Their Necromancer magick poured into their casting hands, making the bones there light up blue. It was something I'd done a thousand times.

Blue light arced from the dead mages' palms, flowing directly into the gateway stones. In the sky, the Martyr's Comet flared a brighter shade of red, casting a crimson glow over the scene. I'd read that the comet bathed the world in red light before it disappeared. Now, I understood why that was so important.

The blue power of the Necromancers mixed with the red energy from the comet, creating a violet colored brightness.

Hybrid magick.

These combined purple lights spread from one gateway to the next, until all the arches blazed with violet light. The long cracks in the earth sealed up before my eyes. The bodies of Not-Elea and Not-Viktor shone with purple light as well.

Then the comet disappeared from the night sky. The brightness that had illuminated Not-Elea and Not-Viktor faded too. As the light left the corpses, the bodies turned more translucent and ghost-like. Within a few seconds, they were completely gone.

For a long moment, the Sire and Lady stared at the spots where the bodies had recently been. The Sire was the first to break the quiet. "I don't like this obsession with hybrid magick. It gets worse with every Elea."

The Lady snapped her fingers. "I have it. Perhaps we should keep them apart next time. If they don't know about each other, they can not work as a team."

The Sire shook his head. "Those two always found each other if they're in the mortal realm, no matter where we placed them. It's like how souls always found us, even before there were gateways."

"In that case, we shall raise the next Viktor with us in the Eternal Realms. We can then place the next Elea with the mortals. We can give her a godling to watch over her when the time comes. As long as she learns the ways of magick eventually, she'll be a great conduit for the gateway."

"Yes." The Sire nodded. "A godling. Tristan would be a fine choice. No woman can resist him."

"Agreed."

I couldn't believe what I'd just seen. The Sire and Lady just admitted that I'd been entrusted to Tristan. Now, I realized the truth. My so-called sacrifice was why I'd been saddled with Tristan's cursed so long ago. It was all so I'd learn Necromancy. After so many years of practice, my body would then automatically channel magick to the gateways.

And it was all for the Sire and Lady.

My blood heated with anger. Where once I had worshipped these two, now I felt nothing but white-hot rage.

The Sire tapped his chin. "Yes, when the time is right, Tristan can force the next Elea to learn how to access her power."

"But there's a flaw in my plan." The Lady sighed. "If the Viktor is raised with us, then he could suss out ways to generate hybrid power using the knowledge of the Eternal Lands. We can't keep him from every library and archive."

"Even if he does learn the secrets of hybrid magick, I doubt a Viktor would become any serious threat. His kind can never take in enough energy." The Sire's voice lowered, and the reverberation shook the ground. "No, an Elea with hybrid power is a far worse worry. If she got the Sword…"

"That will never happen. We'll plan this out perfectly." The Lady clapped her hands. "I have it. You can cast a spell on what's left of the Sword. Turn it into a totem with a possession spell in order to ensure things go smoothly, if all else fails."

"It might not work, considering the Sword isn't whole." The Sire rubbed his chin. "Still, it would act as a failsafe."

"Everything will work out fine. You'll see."

"Yes, my love. You are right. And now, we've other worlds to manage." The word *manage* had an edge to it that set my teeth chattering. One thing was for certain. I wouldn't want to be a resident of any of those worlds.

The Lady looped her hand around the Sire's arm. Meanwhile, a nearby gateway flared with purple light, showing that it was ready to be used. Together, the Sire and Lady stepped through the arch and disappeared.

Once they were gone, I realized a simple fact.

As with Petra, I'd make sure those two paid for what they had done.

CHAPTER SEVENTEEN

After the Sire and Lady departed, my mind spun through everything I knew of Viktor. Threads of facts move themselves into a larger tapestry. My eyes widened with a realization.

I rounded on the ghostly Kila Kitu. "This is why Viktor created the Changed Ones. It's all part of his plan." I scanned the many gateways surrounding the field. They were lined up like so many soldiers, ready to die.

And that's when I truly understood what Viktor had planned.

"Viktor is going to kill the Sire and Lady," I went on. "After that, he'll take over all the gateways. He's already built a mindless army to protect him while he destroys them."

"Yes, I fear that is his plan." Kila Kitu gestured toward my arm. "We should return. You're bleeding out."

"Does that mean you'll give me the Sword?"

"I'm unsure. There's nothing worthy about handing over the hilt, merely to create another tyrant. You're not like my Elea. She was gentle and loving."

"I'm a Grand Mistress Necromancer. Gentle isn't what we're trained to be. And even so…" I opened my mouth, searching for the right words. None came out. Years of Necromancer training made me terrible at conversations like this one. "I've still got, you know, feelings."

What a terrible speech.

Kila Kitu glanced at me from the corner of his eye. I'd seen looks like that one before. It was another way of saying *Sure, you have feelings.*

Another argument appeared. "How about Rowan? He's my mate. That's proof I can love and care for someone."

Kila Kitu gestured toward the sky. "The Martyr's Comet has cycled countless times. In all those eons, you're the only Elea who's found a mate. And your Rowan is a Genesis Rex, no less. You love each other, but your bond is not that strong, is it?"

"I don't know what you mean." I blinked hard, forcing my mind to focus on the present moment. Blood kept dripping from my hand. My head was turning woozy. "Time is running out. You must give me the Sword hilt. I swear, you can trust me."

"How can I rely on you when even your own mate won't? If your bond were true, Rowan would have shared power with you by now. He has not. One tyrant is as bad as the next, and at least, I know what to expect from my current set of ruling fiends."

I opened my mouth again, ready to argue, but Kila Kitu raised his arm toward me. "No. This is over. If you want a way to heal the gateways, use Viktor as the sacrifice."

"I still need the Sword for that. And what are the chances that I'll be able to finish him off right when the Martyr's Comet fades? I can't risk our world in such a foolhardy manner. I need an alternate plan. That's hybrid magick."

"My answer remains the name."

A burst of purple smoke surrounded us. The charge of magick returned to the air. Within seconds, I found myself transported back into the tall round chamber. Nan and Mrefu waited nearby. Meanwhile, the moss and leaf version of Kila Kitu still stood beside me at the center of the stone platform. A pool of my blood encircled us both. On reflex, I pressed my healthy palm against the open wound.

"What happened?" Nan looked up at me from the chamber floor. "Are you all right?" Her eyes widened as she took in the top of the platform. "Where did all this blood come from?"

I squinted, forcing myself to focus on Nan. It wasn't easy. "How long have we been gone?"

"No one went anywhere. One moment you were walking toward Kila Kitu, the next you were standing in a pool of blood." Nan winced. "Is that all yours?"

Mrefu stepped closer, speaking in his strange language. "What did you see?" asked Mrefu. "Can you find the Sword?"

I shook my head, not believing what I was hearing. "Did you just speak to me, Mrefu? And more importantly, did I understand you properly?"

"Yes," said Mrefu. "All who get touched with Kila Kitu's magick become gifted with the power to speak and understand our tongue. How do you think Nan learned?"

The world started to turn hazy at the edges. "I see."

"So, what's the answer Mrefu's question?" Nan turned her attention to Kila Kitu. "Will you give her the Sword's hilt?"

Kila Kitu stood tall, folding his moss arms over his bark-covered chest. "No."

"If that's the case, then there's nothing more she can do here," said a voice. I stilled, knowing that tone as well as I knew my own.

It was Rowan. He was here. Before I left with Kila Kitu, I'd thought someone—or a group—was hiding in the darkness above our heads. Turns out, I was right. Rowan was here, waiting to see if I claimed the Sword.

When my mate spoke again, he broke my heart. "Attack!"

I curled my torn up arm against my chest and tried to focus my hazy brain. With all my concentration, I kept one thought central to my mind.

Escape.

CHAPTER EIGHTEEN

Shadowy figures began scaling down the cavern walls. Rowan and his troops were closing in. The whole scene was turning dream-like, and not only from the fact that I'd lost so much blood.

My mate was coming to attack me.

Moving to stand by my left, Mrefu took out his bow and notched in an arrow. Nan pulled out a dagger and took the spot on my right.

"Cast a spell," ordered Nan.

"I can't. I lost all my memory of incantations. You and Mrefu should run. I can face Rowan alone."

Nan rolled her eyes. "You were always too noble for your own good. I'm not leaving you."

Through the haze in my mind, I managed to speak. "Why do you trust me now?"

"You went with Kila Kitu." Her eyes glimmered. "That took courage. I was wrong to believe Petra's tricks. You'd never order my death behind my back."

I forced a smile. "No, I'd fight you face to face."

"I'm sorry I doubted you." For the first time, I noticed how her skin seemed to shimmer in odd ways in the dim light. There was no time to contemplate that now, though.

Warriors were scaling farther down the walls in their bid to attack us. All my plans were going to implode, right here, unless I could think of something. I scanned my head, desperate for any solution.

Sadly, my mind was as empty as my veins.

With a series of thuds like drumrolls, the first of the warriors reached the chamber floor, their boots hitting the wet ground with a sloshy thud. I should have been planning my escape, but I could only scan the oncoming faces.

Was Rowan in the first group?

I didn't see my mate, but I did spot Kade and Amelia, both wearing their Caster leathers. Kade wielded a sword. Amelia had some kind of cannon contraption winding up her arm. Both of their mouths were contorted into angry snarls.

Was it only a day ago that I'd laughed with Amelia in her laboratory? Or the Casters reached for my fingertips, wishing me well as their best chance to win against Viktor? And now, they all glared at me with outright hatred.

Curse you, Mlinzi and Walinzi.

I was hobbling closer to the edge of the platform when I saw him. *Rowan.* He was everything strong and majestic as he scaled down the wall, a single loop of vine around his right arm.

Then his gaze locked with mine. Nothing but pure rage shone in his green eyes. The sight cut me through, more deeply than any knife.

I had to get out of here.

The only way to get my Rowan back was to find that damnable Sword, and Kila Kitu had it. I rounded on the mage. "I understand that you don't trust me, but you don't trust anyone but your Elea, do you?"

Kila Kitu slowly swung his head from side to side. *No.*

"Well, I'm the closest to her that you'll ever get. And I look like her, don't I?" I gestured toward my face. Kila Kitu winced.

With that, I knew exactly how to get him to give me the Sword.

"Can you really let me go now?" I asked. "Leave me to die like she did?"

Kila Kitu didn't answer, which was a response in itself. He wouldn't leave me to die.

I leaned in closer to him. "If you give me the Sword hilt, I will not betray your trust."

"You do look so much like her," said Kila Kitu in his deep whisper.

"That's right. So give me the hilt. Now. After that, I'll need a way to leave this place safely along with Nan and Mrefu."

Kila Kitu frowned. "You ask too much."

"The hilt is no good to me if I'm imprisoned. Plus, you should want to rescue Nan and Mrefu, they're Zaidi."

All of a sudden, it looked as if the entire cavern were lined with Caster warriors. They raced toward us in a single wave of brown leather and angry faces. I tried to ignore Rowan's glare in the mix.

Kila Kitu gave me the barest of nods. "You are worthy. Barely." With those words, the mage burst back into a swirl of tiny particles. Another vortex appeared on the round platform. Someone gripped my arm through my Necromancer robes. I looked over to see Rowan standing beside me.

"Where is Jicho?" His voice was tight with fury. I could only gape at him in agony and longing.

My Rowan. My mate.

Before I could reply, long tendrils of moss, leaves, and wind wrapped around my body, pulling me into the vortex on the round stage. Rowan was untouched by the gale. Nan and Mrefu quickly became caught in the same whirlwind as well. As the winds moved faster, the stone platform opened up, pulling all three of us underground.

Rowan glared at me from the edge of the pit as I spun lower. It didn't seem possible that our pain and grief could still be so fresh, but it was. My eyes prickled with tears as I spun into the abyss below. In truth, I didn't know where I was going, but at least I was alive. And something even better had come to pass as well: a metal hilt had magickally appeared in my palms. It was made of silver and encrusted with a swirling pattern of tiny amethysts. Kila Kitu had kept his word.

The first part of the Sword of Theodora was mine.

CHAPTER NINETEEN

I didn't know how long I tumbled through the darkness. My fall ended with a jolt. It took me a moment to realize that I'd landed on my feet, in a jungle, and during daytime. Nan and Mrefu were nowhere to be seen. The Sword hilt stayed in my grip, though. After so much pain and loss to get this far, there was no way I was losing it now.

But where was I, exactly? Was this the same place where I'd left Jicho and the *MAJE*?

A voice cut through the dense jungle, answering that question for me. "Elea? Elea?"

My heart soared. That was Jicho.

I could have danced for joy. Kila Kitu had used his magick to drop me off in the jungle right where our metal vessel had been docked. The mage had even made sure I landed on my feet. As magick went, that was rather impressive. I had arrived without Nan or Mrefu, though, which sent pang of loneliness through my soul. It seemed I found friends only to lose them, time and again.

I cupped my hand by my mouth. "I'm here!"

"Don't move," cried Jicho. "I'll get to you." The joy in his voice was unmistakable. It also sounded as if he was speaking from somewhere above my head. I frowned. Had my little friend gone back to climbing trees?

I slipped the hilt into one of the deep pockets of my Necromancer robes. The jungle around me seemed deserted, but I knew enough to realize that was an illusion. Someone could pop out of the shadows at any moment.

Rubbing my neck, I scanned the high branches around me. All of them dripped with vines. There were about a million places a young boy could hide. I tapped my foot, anxious for Jicho to appear. The Casters knew that I'd escaped the cave. It wouldn't take them long to find where I'd gone.

"We're almost there." This time, it wasn't Jicho who was speaking. It was Nan. A weight of worry lifted from my bones. If Nan was with Jicho, then the boy couldn't be in too much trouble.

"I'm ready when you are," I called.

The crackle of magick filled the air. Red mist curled around my feet. My stomach sank. Someone was casting a spell with Caster magick. There was no question who was following me. Rowan. He always was quick with transport spells. And thanks to our mate bond, he could probably cast a tracker spell quickly, too.

A moment later, Rowan materialized before me. "Don't bother trying to run again. You have the Sword hilt, so I'm not letting you out of my sight until I get it." He loomed above me, every muscle in his body coiled with barely held-in fury. "Now, where is my brother?"

My mouth answered before I could stop it. "He's on his way."

"Have you hurt him?"

"Never." I hated how my voice warbled with grief.

Rowan stepped closer. If I leaned forward, I could rest my cheek against his chest. "It's bad enough that you're going after the Sword of Theodora. Who knows what evil you're really up to? But kidnapping my brother? That was a mistake you'll regret."

"I didn't take Jicho. He insisted on helping me find the Sword. He said he had visions—"

"No, you're lying. You must have cast a spell on him to make him follow you."

"Me, a liar? What about you?"

Some of the tension left Rowan's face. "I'm a king. Lies go with the territory."

"So you can lie but not me? And not just any untruth, mind you. You gave me your word that I'd be safe. And yet, you sent your palace mages after me without at least giving me a chance to prove myself." I raised my hand, palm forward. "Just try to share power with me."

Rowan shook his head. "You've cast enough spells on me to last a lifetime. But they've all been played against you, witch. Thanks to your enchantment, I can find you anywhere. Your soul calls to mine."

"That's our mate bond. It's why you can cast tracker spells so quickly." I raised my hand higher. My throat tightened with desire and grief. "Please. Touch me skin to skin with the intent to share power. You'll see."

"I don't know what to make of you sometimes." Little by little, Rowan set his hand on my hip. It wasn't enough to share power—there was still the fabric of my robes between us. Plus there was the intent needed as well. Still the touch was there. It was a start.

My hand trembled as I reached toward my mate, resting my palm against his cheek. Some deep part of my soul instantly felt at rest at the skin-to-skin contact. We still weren't sharing power, but it felt wonderful to be this close again.

"You can't imagine how much I've missed you," I said.

Rowan leaned into my touch. "This defies all logic."

"Now you sound like a Necromancer. A wise man once told me that mate bonds aren't something you can think through. You simply feel them and follow where they go." I would never forget the moment Rowan gave me that advice: it was the night of our bonding ceremony, and I'd been so worried about what it meant that we were connecting and joining power. Rowan had been all things calm and confident.

Feel the mate bond and follow where it goes.

"Some wise man gave you that advice?" The barest gleam shone in Rowan's green eyes. "And who was this brilliant philosopher?"

If I wanted to dance before, I could have jumped with joy now. Rowan was flirting with me. This was beyond wonderful. "It's hard to remember," I said as I wound my fingers behind his neck. "He may have been a king."

Rowan leaned forward until our foreheads touched. "Maybe he still is."

Wings of hope unfurled inside my chest. Rowan was starting to trust in our mate bond, even if he couldn't remember who I was. I wanted to bottle up this moment and savor it forever. Nothing could break the ties between us.

After that, I saw it.

From the corner of my vision, I could just make out a rope ladder dangling through the layers of ferns and wide palm leaves. Nan stood at the bottom rung. Her left arm was looped around the rope while her right beckoned me closer.

She was giving me a way to escape. My breath caught. I couldn't go without Rowan.

"Come with me," I said. "Help me find the rest of the Sword."

Rowan stood up straight again. My hand fell from his neck as he placed more space between us. "That's impossible. Tell me where Jicho is, and I promise, I'll simply let you go. No palace mages or memory spells."

"That's not enough and you know it." I raised my palm again. "Just once. Try."

The happy light drained from Rowan's eyes. "You said it yourself before. I am a king. There are certain risks I simply can't take, and you're one of them."

"What about the Sword?"

"There are other ways to fight Viktor."

"You may be battling far more than Viktor. The Sire and Lady—"

"Please. I'm not foolish enough to think the gods care about the likes of you and me. And I'll never go after some mythical Sword with an enchantress at my side. This isn't a fairy tale."

"We need that Sword."

"No, we don't. What I need is for you to drop this entire farce. This isn't about a Sword or a quest. It's about a false connection. What I told you before? It must be true. You've cast a spell on me."

"I have not. Part of you knows this is the truth.."

"Drop these silly plans for the Sword and disappear back to your own lands. As long as you stay here, I can't guarantee your safety."

"Meaning you'll send your mages after me."

Rowan's voice lowered. "You're going after the Sword of Theodora. That weapon can kill our gods. Our *gods*, Elea."

After what I'd seen with Kila Kitu, Rowan's words heated my blood with rage. I blurted out the first thing that came to mind. "Maybe those *gods* aren't the paragons of virtue you suspect them to be."

"So you admit it. You wish to kill them?" Rowan stepped away from me. "That Necromancer Petra told me that you planned to murder the Sire and Lady, but I thought she was an elderly Mother Superior who was losing her mind."

The moment I heard Rowan's speech, I could have kicked myself. How could I have been so foolhardy? Necromancers don't speak without considering the implications. As a result, Rowan thinks I want to kill the Sire and Lady. "I don't want kill any gods. Only Viktor when he attacks again." *Which he will.*

"Petra doesn't believe you. She says that the gods will take care of Viktor, too."

"And you believe her?"

"I believe that once you have that Sword, there will be a long line of powerful mages trying to take it from you. And yes, with that much magick ready for the taking, I would be one of those mages in line."

I searched Rowan's eyes, trying to see the lie there. Surely, Rowan was merely trying to frighten me. But my mate was telling the truth. If I found the Sword of Theodora, it would have to be without him. And if I succeeded in getting that weapon, he'd become my enemy to boot.

From across the jungle floor, Nan waved at me more fiercely. The motion set the dangling ladder rustling through the leaves.

Rowan stiffened. "What was that?"

There was a moment locked in infinity where I debated what to do next. I could tell Rowan the truth and point out Nan. Rowan respected honestly, but it wouldn't change his decision. On the other hand, I could somehow escape with Nan, but that would only confirm Rowan's suspicions that I was an enchantress out to ruin him and his people.

In the end, there was no choice really. This mission was greater than me and Rowan. To save our people, I had to betray my mate. As fate would have it, Rowan's own brother Kade had taught me what I needed in order to escape.

First, I simply had to have one last kiss.

Going up on tiptoe, I wound my hand behind Rowan's head, feeling the silky scruff of his short-shorn hair under my palm. After that, I kissed him, hard and fast. My soul soared inside me. Down to the very core of my being, I felt a sense of peace at being connected again to my mate.

Yes.

We weren't sharing magick, but the kiss was close enough. I tried to hold onto the feeling before I destroyed it forever.

As our kiss deepened, I moved my hand to Rowan's shoulder. Soon, I hit the very spot Kade had once shown me. It was where, if you applied the right amount of pressure, you could make any mortal collapse. I clamped my fingers onto the right point. Rowan tumbled to the ground, unconscious. Some small part of my being died at the sight.

"Hurry, Elea!" Nan kept up her frantic waving from across the jungle. Rustling sounded in the trees. Someone was heading toward us.

Leaving Rowan behind, I raced toward Nan and her ladder. There was nothing left for it now. I had the hilt and would hopefully find the rest of the Sword soon. In the process, I might lose my heart, but too many people were relying on me across numerous worlds. I couldn't fail them now.

CHAPTER TWENTY

Racing away from Rowan, I quickly reached Nan and her rope ladder. Wrapping my hands around the rough cords, I held the ladder steady as Nan climbed upward.

I shivered, thinking of Rowan's prone body lying on the jungle floor. How did it come to pass that I would hurt my own mate? Shaking my head, I decided not to think about Rowan any more. There was a ladder to climb and—with any luck—once I reached the treetop, Nan had planned some way for us to hide or escape.

Once Nan had scaled high enough to give me room, I began to climb up behind her. I was only a few yards from the jungle floor when it happened.

The ladder began to rise.

And when I say rise, I don't mean that it happened because I was climbing. The entire rope structure lifted up into the trees. Panic tightened every muscle in my body. I clung hard to the rough cords.

"Nan!" I called. "What's going on?"

There was no sense of magick in the air, so whatever this was, it couldn't be a spell. Were there people in the trees hauling us up higher? That didn't seem likely, either. The motion was too smooth for the heave-ho of physical pulling.

"Wait for it," cried Nan. "It'll be glorious."

I didn't have much of a choice, considering. The thought flitted through my mind that this was all some kind of trap from my one-time friend. After all, Nan seemed to change her opinion of me rather rapidly. Back then, I thought it was because I'd faced Kila Kitu, but who knows? Maybe I'd lived through what that mage showed me only to be killed now.

Tree branches and wet leaves smacked against my body as the ladder rose higher and higher. It was an effort to keep my breathing even. I recited every Necromancer meditation I could think of.

"One more moment!" yelled Nan.

I'd have replied, but I was halfway through my mantra of calm. I really didn't need to lose any further focus—the leaves and branches in my face were distraction enough.

After that, we broke through the treetops. What I saw was so shocking I almost lost my grip on the rope ladder.

The *MAJE* had transformed. All those yards of silk in the hull had been blown up into a great balloon that was somehow holding the entire ship aloft. I blinked hard, wondering if the vision before my eyes would change. It didn't.

Jicho leaned over the side of the vessel and beamed a gap-toothed grin. "Wonderful, isn't it?"

I gripped the rope ladder so tightly my knuckles whitened. "It's a bit of a surprise."

"If you'd let me tell you about the *MAJE*, I would have explained. After I finished my story about the bolts. And the metal."

At that moment, an arrow sped by me. Glancing down, I could see the heads and torsos of Caster warriors peeping out from the treetops.

"Better get moving," said Jicho. "Your friends are already on board." He lowered his voice. "They're really nice."

My mind blanked. "My friends?"

Nan then looked out over the edge. "It's me and Mrefu, silly." She rolled her eyes. "I thought you said you were come kind of climbing prodigy."

This entire situation still had me flummoxed. "I was. I am." I'd spent five years learning Necromancy at a mountain cloister. For exercise, I used to climb the rock walls.

Nan rolled her eyes. "Then get your bony arse up here." Another arrow sped by. This one came fairly close to Nan's head. She ducked out of view.

The *bony arse* part jogged my head back into working condition. I scaled up the ladder at top speed. More arrows flew by as I continued my ascent. Within seconds, I reached the MAJE and slipped on deck, landing on my back. Nan, Mrefu, and Jicho all knelt around me.

"Took you long enough," said Nan.

Mrefu let out a grumble. Nan translated.

"And Mrefu says you need to regain your magick soon, since your skills as an athlete are rather poor."

"Mrefu said something? I only heard a grumbling noise." I tilted my head. "I can understand what he says, you know."

Nan winked. "I enhanced things a little."

"Can I tell you about the MAJE now?" asked Jicho.

"Not yet." I couldn't say that without chuckling, however. The boy looked simply too pleased with himself. "We have to get out of here first." In truth, there were a ton of things I wanted to know. What else could this mechanical ship do? Why were Nan and Mrefu along with us? But there wasn't any time, especially because the archers had changed their target away from me.

Rowan's warriors were shooting at the balloon itself.

Great rips sounded as the arrows found their target. Our flying ship lurched, sending me rolling onto a pile of metal tools. I get a few scratches, and that was certainly fortunate. Some of Jicho's tools looked more deadly than knives.

"Right," said Jicho. He turned to one of the panels of gauges and levers that lined the interior of the ship. "We need to get back to the water."

I scanned the distance to the shoreline. "It's close, but we'll make it."

Possibly.

Mrefu, Jicho, Nan and I all crouched on the deck as the MAJE lurched closer to the water.

Thirty yards.

Twenty yards.

Ten.

With a great splash, we landed in the river. Jicho cheered. "We did it!"

I peeked over the stern of the ship. Sure enough, Caster warriors were taking to the water as well. Flashes of crimson light appeared as the mages among them brought sea monsters and flying beasts to life. The warriors took to their mounts. After that, they all took off after me.

The Caster fighters weren't the ones I feared, though. Rowan stood at the edge of the water, staring right at me as red smoke curled around his feet. With our mate bond, he could always find me. And Rowan was nothing if not a master at the transport spell.

If I didn't do something, Rowan would be at my side in a matter of seconds.

I turned to Jicho. "I need to go where Rowan can't transport beside me." A mage would know if a spot was too tight, and they would never transport themselves into a wall. Or in this case, a ship. I gestured along the ship's deck. "Are any of those compartments big enough of for me?"

Jicho pulled open a latch. "Sure, try this one."

"Good. Once I'm hidden, we need to get out of here quickly."

Nan grinned. "You just get below deck and let Nan, Jicho, and Mrefu take care of the rest."

Moving swiftly, I slid into the tiny compartment and snapped the door shut above my head. Nan paced the deck. Although her voice was distant, I could still make out her words as they echoed into my metal chamber. "Crank up that engine. And take the fork to the right."

"Oh, I can see that in my visions," said Jicho. "That's a major waterfall. Perfect."

I rapped on the metal door above me. "Hey, I heard that. How is a waterfall perfect? Don't boats usually avoid those things?"

If anyone heard me, they didn't reply. Instead, I only heard Jicho speaking to Nan and Mrefu. "Over there are some storage compartments big enough for you two. I'll take this one here." The boy's voice sounded far too excited about this for my taste. "No one will follow us past the waterfall. They'll assume we're dead."

"What about Rowan's magick?" asked Mrefu.

"I can see my brother. The transport isn't working. He's casting a Solar Burst now."

"Can you say that in non-mage talk?" asked Nan.

"It's an advanced fireball spell," said Jicho. "He's trying to melt the metal boat, but he doesn't know we're going under water. That fireball will fizzle out the second it touches liquid. Plus, the MAJE can keep us below the river for a short time. Rowan will *really* think we're dead then."

I pounded on the door again. "Jicho, that sounds impossible." I couldn't help but notice how the water was getting choppier. My shoulders were slamming against either wall of the hiding space.

We were definitely heading toward a waterfall.

This time, Jicho answered me. "No, it will be fine. I've had a vision." His voice quivered as he said this, though. In the distance, I could hear the roar of sea monsters and the caw of giant birds. The Caster warriors were closing in. A low voice echoed over the river.

It was Rowan.

He was speaking an incantation. I recognized the words—Jicho was right that it was a Solar Burst. What I didn't have the heart to tell Jicho was that, thanks to our mate bond, Rowan could sense me wherever I went. Sooner or later, he'd figure out that I was alive and know where to find me.

Which wasn't a good thing.

The boat lurched from side to side. The rapids were gaining speed.

"Get below, fast!" cried Jicho. "The boat's ready to dive." A series of slams sounded as Jicho and Mrefu crawled into their hiding spaces.

A soft knock sounded above me. "Elea?"

"Nan? What are you doing? Get below deck."

"Not until I tell you something. I figure we might not live through this, and so I've got to have my say."

I knew Nan well enough to know there was no talking her out of this. "Go on."

"In that battle with Viktor, the one where you raised all those Necromancers? Well, you raised me too. Afterwards, I got another Necromancer to cast a spell and hide the marks. I did it so I could escape Petra. She had agents out who were rounding up anyone with the skull imprint. So, that's why I'm staying with you through this until the end. I owe you my life. And Mrefu owes me his, so you're stuck with both of us."

I rested my palm against the door above my head. My eyes brimmed with tears. "Thank you, Nan."

"Water's coming over the deck. Must dash." With that, I heard the fast beat of her footsteps overhead, followed by another slam as Nan slipped inside her own hiding compartment.

"Get ready!" Jicho's muffled voice sounded from under the metal. "We're almost there!"

Curling up my body into a ball, I wrapped my arms around my head. Hisses sounded as the vessel sealed the compartment to become water-tight around me. I curled up into a ball, my arms wrapped around my knees. Perfect darkness descended into my small space.

Please, let Jicho be right.

The MAJE tilted on its axis. My stomach seemed to hit the roof of my mouth as we plummeted downward. For a moment, I had the illusion of being weightless. After that, my compartment shook as the boat hit the water. We'd fallen. But where?

CHAPTER TWENTY-ONE

After the *MAJE* hit the water, the ship dove downward. A great groan of metal filled the air. My ears popped from the growing pressure. The ship jolted from side to side, throwing me against one metal wall after another.

Then, stillness.

A low hum sounded. Based on what Jicho said, that must be some kind of propulsion system that was moving us through the water. I leaned back against the metal wall and exhaled.

We'd made it this far.

After that, the vessel tilted upward. We were heading back toward the surface once more. Jicho's automatic pilot certainly worked. Even so, other parts of the ship didn't fare as well. Water seeped in through the seams in my small chamber. Once we reached air, the hatch above me popped open. I scrambled out and scanned the deck of the ship. Jicho, Nan, and Mrefu were all crawling out of their respective hiding places.

Safe. We'd all made it.

Rising to stand, I scanned our surroundings. The river here was faster as it cut through heavier jungle. Vines and trees arched over the water, allowing only a thin glimpse of sky through the green.

Early morning. About one day left.

The *MAJE* was afloat and coasting along with the current. Other than that, the boat was a smashed-up mess. The top "fin" had been torn off. Its sleek cylinder engine was now a crushed up hulk. And the shark appearance of the vessel was completely gone. The thing more resembled a crumpled-up wad of metal parchment.

Still, we were all alive.

I carefully inspected the river behind us. *No sign of Rowan, either.* In my mind, I knew that was a good thing. My heart, however, ached to see him once more and console him. The look of despair and grief on his face as we sped away? It was something I'd carry with me forever.

Jicho's small hand wrapped around my own. "Are you all right?"

I knelt so I could face the child directly. "I am fine. You did a great job helping us escape."

Jicho's big green eyes widened with sympathy. "He'll remember you again, Elea. You're his mate."

I wrapped the boy in a too-tight hug before realizing that Nan and Mrefu were staring. At this point, I either needed to explain the history with Rowan or move onto other topics. Fortunately, there are other subjects that I desperately want to discuss.

I stepped back from Jicho and tried to regain my composure. "How far until we reach the place where the Sword's blade is hidden?"

Jicho's mouth fell open. "You have the hilt?"

I patted my pocket. "I do."

"The blade isn't far now," said Nan.

"That's right," added Jicho. He wouldn't meet my gaze. "I saw it in a vision, really."

"That's great, Jicho." I tilted my head and scanned everyone carefully. There was something going on here that I was missing.

As if on cue, Nan and Mrefu exchanged a knowing look.

I leaned back to sit on the deck. "Seems like we have some time now. How about someone tell me where this Sword is and what to expect? I get the feeling like you all know."

"I've been to this place before," said Nan. "It was pretty rough."

"She was tested," added Mrefu.

"Tested how? Battle testing?"

"I can't tell you that." Nan plunked down onto the deck and wrapped her arms around her legs. "Wish I could."

Deciding to try another tactic, I focused on Jicho. "Have you had any visions lately?"

"A few."

"Do you know if we'll see Rowan and the Casters again before we reach the hiding place of the blade?"

Jicho paused. "No, we won't. He's with the Lady now."

"The Lady of Creation?" I couldn't believe what I was hearing. "Is she hurting him?"

"She's giving him a choice."

"And what is that choice, exactly?"

Jicho looked up from his controls. "I can't tell you that, Elea." His normally happy face was the definition of miserable. "I'm sorry. It's how things work when you're a Seer. You can't tell everything you want to." His bottom lip wobbled. "All I can say is that we're going to a temple, and that Rowan loves you. Let him help you."

Guilt pressed in around me, tight as a vise. Sweet Jicho. He was being so brave in a terrible situation. I shouldn't keep pushing. I scanned the ship, seeing how Nan and Mrefu had begun opening the remaining container spaces. Most were damaged and empty, but others still held supplies. Whenever they found some food or equipment, they set it on deck.

I cleared my throat. "I'll just help Nan and Mrefu for a while."

Rolling up my sleeves, I began assisting my friends in their work. If nothing else, I knew that I wouldn't see Rowan again until we reached the temple. I couldn't wait.

CHAPTER TWENTY-TWO

Mrefu and I organized what remained of the *MAJE's* supplies. As the hours passed, the jungle grew more dense.

A thick nest of vines, ferns, and trees blotted out all but the occasional view of the sky. In fact, most of the time I couldn't stand up without my hair catching on a branch or fern. I ended up sitting on deck, my legs pulled against my chest, feeling lonely and miserable. No one spoke, and the silence became its own kind of cacophony.

In this way, we all passed the hours until Jicho finally spoke. "We're close."

I shifted to peep over the edge of the vessel. Sure enough, the jungle outside the boat was changing. Along the shoreline, random clumps of vines now took on a more linear edge. All that natural greenery was covering up something made by humans. Over the past hours, I was starting to suspect that Nan and Mrefu at least knew the name of the temple, but had promised Jicho not to tell me. I decided to test out that theory now.

"That's a wall," I said. "We must be getting closer to the temple of—"

I waited for someone to complete the phrase, but Jicho, Nan, and Mrefu merely exchanged sad glances.

That had been happening more and more lately.

I straightened my shoulders. *So what did it matter if an awful fate awaited me?* I'd faced down my share of evil, and the best approach was simply to get it over with. I turned to my shipmates.

"What's the fastest way to the temple?" I asked.

No one answered.

I shifted my gaze between Nan and Mrefu. "Come on. I know you both are aware of this place somehow."

"It's a sacred spot to the Zaidi," said Mrefu. "I brought Nan here soon after I owed her my life. It's where she was tested."

"Up ahead, there's a place where we can tie up," said Nan. "After that, the temple is a short walk away."

Nan was talking again, so I decided to push for more information. I was nothing if not persistent. "What was your testing like?"

Nan couldn't meet my gaze. "Not easy." She exhaled a long breath. "You'll see for yourself soon enough."

Along the riverside, the ferns and vines receded, revealing a low wall made of brown stone. Heavy loops of bronze had been hammered into the rock, creating many places for vessels to tie up. At one point, this must have been a busy spot. However, those days were long gone. Based on all the overgrowth blocking the river, no one had been here for ages.

Jicho secured the vessel to the pier with loops of heavy rope. From the corner of my eye, I saw a face in the recesses of the jungle. My body froze with excitement.

It was Rowan.

And nothing less than a miracle was taking place, because Rowan was looking right at me while smiling his lopsided grin. My soul felt so light it was as if I could soar to the clouds.

On reflex, I leapt off the boat and onto the muddy shore. Some small part of me thought it was strange that Nan, Jicho, and Mrefu didn't comment about my running off. In fact, they didn't even seem surprised that Rowan was here. My three shipmates simply watched me leave, despair dimming their eyes.

I couldn't find it in myself to care.

"Listen, Elea—" Jicho started to call to me, but Nan shushed him. Normally, I'd stop and ask Jicho what he meant. However this situation was anything but normal. At long last, my mate had recognized me again. Had the Lady returned his memory? A girl could hope.

Still smiling, Rowan waved me toward him. Then he paused, turned, and ran off into the jungle. My mate hadn't said anything, but the message was clear all the same.

I love you, Elea.

Come follow me.

I took off into the darkened jungle at a run.

CHAPTER TWENTY-THREE

I rushed off into the jungle. Long branches tugged at my robes, pulling me backward. Wet earth sloshed around my feet, slowing my every step. From above, thin tendrils of vines snagged my hair. All around, everything seemed focused on a single purpose: keeping me from my pursuit of Rowan.

It wouldn't work. The more I was impeded, the harder I pushed myself to run. Still, it didn't matter how quickly I sped forward. Rowan always remained too far ahead to touch.

Even so, I didn't mind.

This was my love.

And he was smiling.

Some small corner of my mind cried out that this was all an illusion. The sense of magick was thick in the air. Plus, the edges of Rowan's body shimmered, like this wasn't his true self so much as his soul. Even so, my heart was too thrilled to bother with reality. And let's not forget the Lady! She had untold powers. Perhaps she gifted me with the sight of Rowan's soul for her own purposes.

Whatever the reason, these few moments of magick and love might be all the happiness I had left to share with Rowan.

I was taking them.

Laughing, I kept running after my mate. Each time he glanced over his shoulder and beamed, I soaked up that crooked grin as if it were the last time I'd ever see it.

It very well might be.

The jungle receded around us. I hardly noticed the change. Soon, great walls made of brown brick rose up on either side of me. The muddy earth under my feet gave way to a checkerboard pattern of stone. None of that mattered. All I knew was that as the jungle receded, I could see more of my mate.

We reached a large chamber. Statues lined the walls, all of them life-sized and incredibly detailed, having been made of bronze, wood, and stone. Hundreds of dolly-mechs lined the floor, all of them standing in groups of three. In each case, there was a man and a woman kneeling before a standing figure whose face was covered with a drawn hood. Behind the dolly-mechs, the chamber walls were filled with arches that were also made of stone, bronze, and wood. I thought back to the Meadow of Many Gateways. This space reminded me of that spot—from the checkerboard ground to the many gateways—but that's where the similarities ended. There certainly hadn't been any statues.

There was no time to wonder more about the temple interior, however. Rowan had slowed his pace as he closed in on the massive gateway set into the far wall of the long rectangular space.

Something about that arch set my teeth on edge.

Up until now, I'd been enjoying this game of pretend with an illusion of my mate. But even though I was excited, my mind wasn't so shut off that I couldn't wonder at this mystery.

Was this all some way to capture me?

I rubbed my neck and thought through the possibilities. In the end, it didn't matter if this was a trap. From what Kila Kitu told me, the rest of the Sword of Theodora was hidden in this temple, and my mate's soul was leading me to it. I had to take a closer look.

After taking in a slow breath, I stepped toward the largest gateway. This massive arch was like everything else in this temple: a mixture of bronze, wood, and stone. In this larger gateway, the three materials had been fashioned into hefty gears that formed the arch's edge.

How odd. Most gateways were lined with gemstones, not clockwork. That meant something, but at the moment, I couldn't place what. Still, I slowed my pace. Intuition told me that Rowan was about to do something.

A memory appeared in my mind: Nan, Mrefu, and Jicho frowning at one another as we tied up the *MAJE* nearby. They all knew what sad fate awaited me. Perhaps this was the moment things would turn sour.

I paused a few yards away.

Rowan touched the arch's frame. The gears spun. Metal creaked. Stone split. On the right-hand side of the gateway, a piece of metal materialized into a section of gears.

It was gleaming.

Sharp.

The blade of the Sword of Theodora.

And it was set right into the wall.

Rowan turned to me. "You have the hilt. If you promise me one thing, then the blade will magickally break free from the wall. The entire Sword will be yours."

I stepped closer. In every way, this man looked like my mate: green eyes, strong build, and worn Caster leathers. But he was still surrounded by a sheen of white light. Magick stayed thick in the air. I'd seen soul spells before. I'd cast them, too. At closer range, I could tell this was indeed my mate's spirit. This Rowan recognized me. His soul in its pure form would always know its mate. And if my mate knew who I truly was, he would never hurt me.

I glanced longingly at the exit archway. *Or would he?*

Rowan gave me his crooked smile once more. "I know what you're thinking. My sweet Elea, still unsure whether to fully trust anyone. Even me."

"I'm trying."

Crowned

"As am I." Spirit-Rowan stared at his hand. "If only my mortal form would believe in our bond enough to touch you with the intent to share power, then all of this might have ended differently. I'd do anything to spare you pain, my mate."

It was such a Rowan thing to say, that my eyes began to sting with held-in tears. "It's really you, isn't it?"

"This is my soul. After you escaped from me, the Lady summoned my spirit to the Eternal Lands. In this form, I can remember everything. I know who you are and what must happen."

"What exactly did the Lady tell you to do?" I tried to control my tone, but I couldn't help the note of disbelief that wove through the question.

"Does it matter? This is my true self, and I'm here to ask you a question."

My pulse raced so quickly, my heart felt like a hummingbird was trapped inside me. "Go on."

"Will you promise me one thing?"

"What?"

"The Sword of Theodora can slay anything."

"Yes. That's why we need it. It can kill Viktor without hurting anyone else." *Like me.* Viktor had shown me once that when he was cut, I'd bleed as well.

"It can kill a spirit as well, you know."

My breath caught. "You don't mean—"

"You must promise to kill my soul right now. That would end my body, too." Spirit-Rowan got down on his knees and bowed his head, exposing the back of his neck.

I'd seen that pose before. *On the Meadow of Many Gateways.* Not-Elea had crumpled onto her knees so the executioner could destroy her. Even worse, Not-Elea had been blackmailed into giving up her life in exchange for those she loved. And now this same trick was being used on me in reverse.

In my case, I wasn't going to kneel, not even metaphorically.

"No, Rowan. Never."

"But this is what must happen. It's what always happens. Someone must recharge the gateways and heal our realm. I won't

161

let it be you. Give me this. Allow me to spare you the pain. Kill my soul and release the power."

"No, you have it all wrong." I pounded my chest with my fist. "I'm the Elea here. Not you. I have the hybrid power for the gateways."

"Do you?" Rowan looked up until emerald gaze locked with mine. "And yet, I still have your power within me, remember?"

My veins chilled as I realized the truth. "That's right. When we were back at the Skullock Passage—right before I spied on the gods—I gifted you so much power. You're still filled with hybrid energy. Is it enough?"

"The Lady thinks so. Without the memory of you, I haven't known what to do with it. Right now, my mortal form doesn't even know I have hybrid magick within me, let alone how to release the power. That's why this is the perfect solution. Now, I can protect you. I'm begging you. Let me help you."

I popped my hand over my mouth. That's just what Jicho had said. *"Let him help you."*

But to allow Rowan to die, body and soul? The thought made my ill. "You don't mean that," I said slowly. "You cannot want me to kill you."

"I do mean it." His gaze stayed locked with mine, intense and determined. "This is the only way."

Every corner of my soul recoiled at his words. "No. There has to be another option. I saw Kila Kitu use hybrid magick to activate a gateway. There must be some means to use it to heal the gateways, too. If only the gods would let us try a few experiments..."

"That's not possible, even if enough time remained. We are infected with hybrid power. It will corrupt us, sooner or later."

"But what about Skullock Passage? Remember when you set me free from the gateway? Cords of purple light and power wound up your arm. I've been thinking about those quite a bit. Maybe that's the key to our spell."

"The gods needed eons to master hybrid magick and gateways. *Gods*, Elea. What can we do in a matter of seconds or minutes? We must live out our destiny."

"The Sire and Lady are powerful entities, but they aren't all-knowing beings." I couldn't help the edge of anger to my voice. "You don't know what they're capable of. Some of the worlds they rule call them tyrants. Mlinzi and Walinzi can't stand them."

"Mlinzi and Walinzi, you mean the trickster gods who stole my memories as well as your ability to cast spells?"

"They're tricksters. It's what they do. But I believed them when they told me about the Sire and Lady. The beings you call gods have turned sour. It's why their hybrid magick went rotten and they can't charge up the gateways themselves."

"No, it's like I told you. Hybrid magick always corrupts."

"I've met the Zaidi," I said. "They wield hybrid magick and have never turned into bubbling tar monsters."

"And I met the Lady of Creation," countered Rowan. "She told me these things herself. We have to follow her plan."

I folded my arms over my chest. I couldn't believe this was coming down to a war of words with some missing deity. "The Lady spoke to you, eh? So why isn't she here to tell us this?"

"The Sire and Lady aren't like us. The rules of appearing and disappearing vary for them. As I told you, the Lady pulled my soul to her realm and that's where we spoke. I truly believe what she had to say."

I knelt before Spirit-Rowan. "Listen, I don't want to die here. And I won't murder you, either. We can use our hybrid power to heal these gateways. That's what I believe."

Rowan stared at me for a long moment. At last, he spoke again. "And what about Viktor?"

My heart sped. If Rowan was asking me questions, it meant he was considering what I had to say. I was convincing him. I began speaking in rapid-fire style. "Viktor wants to kill the Sire and Lady and take their place. I'm naturally stronger with hybrid magick, but Viktor learned some tricks too. That's why he created the Changed Ones and drained Necromancers. It's why he created that army."

"All the more reason for me to die. The Lady explained it all to me. Once the arches are recharged, there is no more reason for Viktor to plot and scheme. The balance of our realms will be restored. If we don't heal the gateways, our very world will fall apart. Then, everyone will perish."

"No, we can use our hybrid magick on the gateways." My voice shook. "At least, we can try."

"How? My mortal form still doesn't remember you. We can't go back to the way things were."

"Of course, we can." I pulled the hilt from my pocket and pointed to the blade set into the wall. "You can release that blade, can't you?"

"It's held by a spell. The blade will be released once you promise to heal the gateways, either with your life or mine."

"I refuse to accept that." I pointed at the stretch of wall that held the rest of the Sword of Theodora. "I will find another way to get that blade and once I do, I'll reform this Sword. There's other magick at work here. Mlinzi and Walinzi promised me that once I had the full Sword in my hands, I'd be able to cast again and you'd regain your memories. We're so close to being able to fight for our future. That's worth fighting for, isn't it?"

"Things have gone too far, Elea. There's so much you don't know."

I didn't like the resigned look on Rowan's face. "What do you mean?"

"Viktor is imprisoned on the other side of this gateway." Rowan gestured behind him. "This arch is the most important one for hybrid magick to recharge, and the longer we delay, the closer Viktor gets to figuring out how to escape again."

I stared into the gateway. Under the arch, white curls of smoke twisted in perfect spirals. *Magick.* And it wasn't purple, blue, or red in shade. This was someone else's power entirely. And since it was coming out of the gateway where Viktor was exiled? He truly was about to break through.

"Viktor is right behind this very arch? How is you dying a good plan?"

"This is the Lady's scheme. She wanted to place you right before Viktor's gateway so you can see how dire things have become. You must promise to wield the Sword now. This is what it means to be a ruler. We make sacrifices."

I hadn't heard Nan, Jicho, and Mrefu enter the temple, but then again, I hadn't been paying much attention to anything but Spirit-Rowan. Now, I could sense them steal up to stand beside me. My gaze skipped between each of their faces. "You knew this was coming, didn't you?"

"You are being tested," said Jicho. "I've seen it from the beginning."

"Everyone who steps into the temple is given a choice," added Nan. "You must do what's right."

I stared at the blade in the wall, my mind whirling through options and plans. Back on the *MAJE*, Nan had said she came here before to be tested. And Jicho had said that Rowan would want what was best for me. Was Rowan's own brother asking me to kill him?

"I can't kill my mate," I said simply.

"But I've seen you take up the blade," said Jicho. "You kill Rowan's spirit here in this temple. I hate it, but it's what has to happen."

"Don't forget, that's what Rowan's soul wants too," added Nan.

Mrefu added his thoughts into the mix. "Kila Kitu trusted you to do what is right. Promise your life or Rowan's. Set the hilt onto the blade and the magick will release it. It's the only way to recharge the gateway and prevent Viktor's invasion."

When I spoke again, my voice was a hoarse whisper. "No."

"But I want you to do this," pleaded Spirit-Rowan. "My conscious self knows nothing, yet my soul realized what must be done. That's what the Sword has always been purposed for. Look around you."

For the first time, I really scanned my surroundings. The dolly-mechs stood in clusters of three. In each case, it was the same two figures who knelt on the ground. My eyes widened with recognition.

There were many Eleas who were not me.

And many Viktors who were not Viktor.

In all, there were hundreds of variations of our faces and bodies. Kila Kitu said this had happened for thousands of years. How many of us had died for the Sire and Lady?

Behind each kneeling pair stood another figure in a long bronze cloak, the hood drawn low to hide their face.

"I see you still do not believe," said Spirit-Rowan. "Show her."

With those words, the dolly-mechs came to life. With a series of clicks, all the versions of me and Viktor bowed their heads. The figure behind them raised a bronze version of the Sword of Theodora high.

That person was the executioner.

And in this moment, Spirit-Rowan wanted that executioner to be me.

My heart railed against the idea. I gripped the hilt more tightly in my palm. "I told you. I will make this Sword whole again." I stalked up to the wall and set the hilt against the base of the blade. It slipped into place with a soft click. After that, I tried to pull the Sword from its holding place in the wall. For the trickster's spell to be broken, I needed to fully grasp the sword

And so I tried.

And tried.

My fingertips became bloody with the effort. I wouldn't give up, though. Closing my eyes, I summoned fresh magick into my body. I couldn't cast a spell, but enhancing my strength never needed an incantation. Back on the farm, I'd used magick to help chop wood and scare off suitors. Now, I'd use the same power again, only to end this insane cycle. Within seconds, the bones in my arms glowed with indigo-colored light.

Perfect.

Raising my fists high, I slammed them against the stone, bronze, and wood of the gateway. Blue sparks exploded everywhere. For a time, there was nothing but my fury, the Sword, and the gateway.

CRASH!

Great cracks formed in the arch. The Sword was still intact, but the gateway was splintered. Gears that had lain flat against the wall now sat at odd angles. Spirit-Rowan's body glowed more brightly than ever before.

Then he disappeared.

Panic streamed through my limbs. "Rowan!"

As if in response, white spirals of magick came to life under the gateway. I gasped. Viktor. Had he been waiting here this entire time, looking for his chance to strike?

Beams of pearlescent light poured out from the gateway, twisting across the floor like so many snakes. The sense of magick became so thick, the air sparkled with its power. Quick as a whip, the cords of bright light wound Nan, Mrefu, and Jicho. The three froze in place for a moment. After that, they all collapsed to the ground. I rushed over and checked them.

All of them were in an enchanted sleep.

Another flare of white light pulsed from the gateway. Sure enough, a tall man appeared on the other side. Like always, he had lean features and dark robes. My insides twisted with fear and hate.

Viktor was here.

I wanted to tell him a thousand things. How he'd made so many mages suffer with his experiments. What he'd done to my life with his insane curse. That he had no right to touch Rowan's soul. The only thing I got out was a single word. "You."

"Yes, me." Viktor's lean features twitched with rage. "That was a rather entertaining scene. I enjoy watching you fret over nonsense. You want to know a secret?"

"No."

"Ah, but you're lying. Do you know how I can tell?"

I shook my head. Still, a burst of white mist poured out from the gateway, settling against my skin to encase me in a thin sheen of magick. My body froze. I could no longer leave the spot or look away. It was another form of possession spell, just like what had been cast on Echo, only this one controlled only my body but not my mind.

"I know everything about you," said Viktor slowly. "Because you are my very own sister." He waved me toward him. "Sending magick outside the gateway is massive drain on my power, and I must conserve my energy for what is to come. Enter into my realm and I'll tell you all about my plans."

Viktor stepped off into the light that streamed from under the gateway. Meanwhile, Nan, Jicho, and Mrefu remained in their enchanted sleep. For my part, I tried to run away, but my limbs wouldn't obey the commands from my brain. My skin still gleamed with the power of Viktor's spell, confirming the fact that I was trapped.

Once again, I mentally cursed those damned trickster gods. "What I would do to be able to cast a counter-spell."

Even so, there was no point dreaming about incantations. Thanks to the possession spell, my body had no choice but to heed Viktor's demands, and so I followed him into the ethereal light.

CHAPTER TWENTY-FOUR

Stepping through the gateway, I found myself in a space made entirely of white light. Brightness stretched off in every direction; there wasn't even a horizon line. Only one figure stood out in full color: Viktor. He loomed over me in his long Necromancer robes, the drawn-out features of his pale face set into a mask of false calm. Deep in his eyes, there burned an inferno of rage.

Viktor bowed slightly to me. "Let us speak of the truth here. You owe that to me, at the very least."

"I owe you nothing."

His pinched face radiated a single emotion: rage. "Do you see this horrid prison you locked me in? You've no idea what a terror it is to be limited to monotonous brightness."

I suppressed the urge to roll my eyes. "Terror? Being here is far less terrible than having your magick drained until you're dead. Or having your arm ripped off and replaced with that of an animal familiar."

"I did what I had to in order to survive. Gathering Necromancer magick into myself is essential for the upcoming war with the Sire and Lady. And I simply had to have an army."

"You talk about destroying Necromancer and Caster lives like it was nothing."

"Isn't it? You and I are special. We live by different rules."

As it turned out, Viktor isn't the only one who could scowl with proficiency. "I am not your sister."

"Don't be thick. Didn't you ever wonder if we were related? By now, you've surely seen the versions of us throughout history."

I paused. Were Viktor and I indeed related? I turned the idea over in my mind; it didn't seem possible. "My only parent was my guardian Rosie. You are no brother to me. You forced me here with a possession spell to spew nothing but lies."

"And how do you suggest I demonstrate the sincerity of my actions now?"

"Free me from this possession."

"Done." Viktor waved his arm. The bright lights faded from my skin and I could move freely once more. There was no question about the first thing I wanted to do with my new-found mobility. I gestured to the gateway behind me. I couldn't see anything beneath the arch, but I knew Mrefu, Nan, and Jicho were magickally asleep on the temple floor beyond. "And what about my friends?"

Viktor shrugged. "They're not possessed, obviously."

"That's not what I meant."

"Oh, you mean their lives. They will be perfectly safe." Viktor waved his hand. "Now that I've proven myself in good faith, how about we talk a while?"

"No." I started to turn away.

Viktor sighed. "Fine. Walk away. Be my guest. While you're at it, keep living in ignorance about who you are and what you can do."

I hated myself for listening to the man. And I loathed the fact that I didn't have a quick response to what Viktor had to say. But most of all, I couldn't stand the fact that he was actually making some sense. If I was going to heal the gateway, then I did need to understand hybrid magick. Unfortunately, Viktor wielded it well enough to create the Changed Ones. He might be able to help.

Turning again, I stared into the face of a man that—if I were being absolutely honest with myself—could very well be my brother. Viktor had killed and tortured thousands of mages. Doing anything with him was a terrible idea. But Viktor also held some valuable information. In the end, there really was no choice about what to do next.

"What do you want, Viktor?"

"Glad to see you're ready to discuss some unpleasant realities. I'm impressed. Let's chat about our parents, shall we?"

"My parents are already dead."

"No, *our* parents are alive. We're the children of none other than the Sire of Souls and the Lady of Creation."

My head turned foggy as I thought through every memory of my childhood. I never knew my parents. The reports of their death were just that: writings on sheets of parchment. Even so, it seemed impossible. "We are not their children."

"Odd to think of them as having limitations, but when they reproduce, they always create twin offspring, a boy and girl, and we continually look rather similar."

I pinched the bridge of my nose. Foul as this news was, it did make sense. "You were raised in the Eternal Lands. That's why you knew how to go back and forth through gateways."

"Doesn't every child learn how to sneak out of the house? And yet, they had you raised on earth to become more compliant. That didn't work now, did it? You're rather bullheaded. But their schemes did succeed in one respect. It was good for you that I didn't know you existed, otherwise I'd have drained your powers as an infant. No offense meant. I simply like to drain things of magick."

My body felt numb. "This doesn't seem real. The Sire and Lady are my parents." There were so many times I'd yearned to know them.

"You have my pity, sister mine. I can't imagine the cruel heart that would plant their own child with a human guardian. Plus, they took no interest in you until you came into your powers. And only then, they wished you to train In Necromancy so you could one day power their precious gateways."

His words cut into my soul. Indeed, I had spent many years trying to squeeze my life into that of a farm girl merely because I thought that was what my parents would have wanted. All the while, they only wanted to fatten up my powers so they could destroy me. "So, we share loathsome parents. Not sure how that matters now."

"On the contrary, I think it's quite important. Our parents are horrid beings. Hybrid magick always goes sour with them. However, with you and that little Creation Caster king—"

"Leave Rowan out of it."

A malicious gleam lit up Viktor's eyes. "Again, she proves herself to be the blundering fool. Aren't you even going to *pretend* that dolt isn't your weak spot? Do you know nothing of how other Eleas have been manipulated into giving up their lives?"

I kept my features perfectly calm, which was a bit of an achievement. "Why don't you just tell me what you want from me?"

"It's a good thing you got more natural hybrid magick ability, dear sister, because you're a bit dim in the brains department. I figured out how to manipulate hybrid power in a mere ten years. It took our parents twenty millennia."

"As I recall, you were raised in the Eternal Lands. I'm sure that helped a little. Doesn't the Sire of Souls—I mean, our father—have quite the extensive library?"

Viktor cleared his throat. "That doesn't matter." Even so, I could tell by the angry gleam in his eyes that it mattered quite a lot.

"So you say."

Viktor lifted his chin. "It comes down to this. I plan to kill our parents and take their place. I want your help."

"I'd rather you took my place in the gateways, honestly."

"But you know that's not an option. Setting me loose…Getting the Sword…And then, I'd have to deliver the right provocation at the precise moment for you to be justified in killing me.

You're too noble for your own good. That's why I need you. I'll protect you from yourself. Give up on this dream of using hybrid magick to heal the gateways."

I rubbed my neck, thinking. "I don't see how I'm necessary to your plans. You have an army. You control hybrid magick. You could kill the Sire and Lady and then heal the gateways yourself."

"Consider it my brotherly love for you. I wish you and your Caster boy to take part in my ultimate success."

I slowly eyed my brother. Every line of his body concealed tightly-held rage. He was furious with the very concept of demeaning himself to speak to me. There was no brotherly love here. If Viktor wanted my help, there could be only one reason why he sought it. Not love. Power.

"In other words," I said slowly. "You aren't strong enough to heal the gateways on your own. You need Rowan and me."

"I need no one!" bellowed Viktor. "I'm offering you the chance of many lifetimes! If you don't team with me, then our parents will sacrifice you and heal the gateways. I'll still get the Sword and kill them."

"But you won't be able to rule everywhere, will you? If our parents heal the gateways with me, then they rule those worlds. But if you get me to be your sacrifice, then the empire falls to you, doesn't it? Or am I too thick to understand what you want here?"

"I try to be a good brother, and this is what happens."

"Oh, did my doltish mind figure out something on its own? How horrible of me. You don't just want our parents dead. You want to rule all the known worlds." I sniffed. "You'd think patricide and matricide would be satisfying enough."

Viktor stepped closer, his body positively vibrating with fury. "Make no mistake. You need me. I know the spells our parents cast particular in order to stabilize the Meadow of Many Gateways. You won't be able to succeed without me."

"You know the spells? Prove it. Name one."

Viktor looked away for the barest second. It was a quick glance, but it had liar written all over it. "I don't have to prove myself to you."

"Do you don't know how to wield hybrid magick and heal the gateways. How disappointing."

Viktor waved his arm dismissively. "You're wrong about my requiring you and Rowan for power. I drained thousands of Nec-romancers and Casters, pulling their energy into my own body. I have plenty of magick to heal the gateways."

"This sounds familiar. Great claims and no proof. Go on. Show me."

"I don't know what you mean."

"You want my help? Pull some hybrid magick into your palm. Prove to me that you're not doing this because you need my power, but because you love me as a sister."

Viktor kept glaring at me, his nostrils flaring with every breath. At length, he spat out one word. "Fine." Pulling up his long sleeve, Viktor exposed his right arm. Within a few seconds, this palm began to glow with violet light.

"See?" said Viktor. "I can wield this power easily. We are done here."

I raised my pointer finger. "Let's give this one more minute." I stepped in for a closer look. Sure enough, a puff of smoke engulfed his hand. *More magick.* Viktor's skin quickly transformed from a pale sheet of flesh into a bubbling glob of tar-like ooze. I lowered my hand. "As I suspected. You need me."

"I need nothing!" Viktor's face flushed. "Do you know what will happen at the end of this Martyr's Comet? You'll die anyway."

"That may be, but I'll tell the Sire and Lady all about you first."

"Really?" Viktor chuckled, and it was a chilling sound. "I'll let you in on a secret. Those two got rather attached to me, raising me themselves and all. Right now, they see me as the reformed son. I've spent my days meditating here in this empty world. As a result, I've officially seen the error of my ways."

"They can't really think that."

"They're like anyone else. They believe what they want to believe. Besides, my transgressions are nothing compared to yours. I tried to harness a bit of hybrid power. I stored a scintilla on some insects that I left lying around. I channeled a little more into some Changed Ones. But yes, I'll admit it. You are right. My abilities are nothing compared to the power you and Rowan could wield. Hybrid magick with a human mage. It's quite a trick. I tried it, you know. A mate bond with a mortal."

"Tristan told me that you had a mate."

"It was a failed experiment, I'll admit that too. My connection with Hannah wasn't like anything like what you have with Rowan. We could barely share a whit of power. When our parents found out, they determined that my so-called mate had to die. Those two are terrified of the kind of mate bond you've already forged. In the end, I put up a good show of weeping and carrying on at Hannah's execution. Despite their shortcomings, our parents are still rather protective of our feelings while we're alive."

"You watched Hannah die?"

Viktor lifted one shoulder. "It was for the best. I needed to give up on my mate bond tests and consolidate my power in other ways. Hannah's death led to my experimentation with Bone Crawlers and ultimately, to success."

Bile crawled up my throat. "You have a strange definition of success."

"Do I? Once you recharge the gateways, I'll grab the Sword of Theodora, kill our parents, and rule this realm. True, it's not as exciting as ruling every world with sentient life. Still, as consolation prizes go, it isn't terrible." Viktor's eyes lit up with pure rage. "And I'll have the extra joy of watching you die."

Images flashed in my mind. The Meadow of Many gateways. Me on my knees with the bronze-robed figure above me. Viktor watching on with delight, ready to kill our parents. Did I really think I'd learn enough about hybrid magick to heal the gateways on my own? Wasn't I better off teaming with Viktor? That way, at least I'd be sure that Rowan and I survived.

"I can see that you're considering it." Some of the tightness and rage seeped out of Viktor's face.

I sighed. "There's still a half day before the Martyr's Comet disappears."

"Meaning you'll figure out something else, since you have so much time."

"Wouldn't you in my case?"

"Obviously. Activate." A flash of energy pressed through the air. A totem ring on Viktor's hand had come to life. My brother had just cast a spell.

"What did you do?"

"Awarded my birthday gift for you, dear sister." The way he said the *dear sister* part, the words dripped with malice. I had the overwhelming desire to run for cover. "Consider my offer carefully. It's the only way for you and your Caster pet to get out of this catastrophe alive. In fact, as a sign of good faith, I'll do you a favor now. When you leave here, I'll make one of the gateways light up and show you a vision of your physical, non-ghostly Rowan. You can merely gaze upon his manly beauty under the arch or step through to see him. Your choice."

Some small part of me was tempted to say thank you. After all, I would enjoy seeing Rowan in a gateway even if I didn't step through it. Still, I doubted that whatever Viktor was doing would truly be a favor to me. My brother was evil to the core. "Goodbye, brother."

"Remember my offer, dear sister."

As I stepped back out of gateway, I realized that Viktor had pulled me inside in order to convince me to follow him, but instead he gave me critical information. Viktor confirmed that Rowan and I wielded enough hybrid power to heal the gateway, and that it's also possible to do so.

Mlinzi and Walinzi's promise echoed in my thoughts. Once I had the Sword in my hands, Rowan and I would get our memories back. And then, if the tricksters' promises held true, that would be the moment when I'd also know exactly how to wield hybrid magick to heal the gateways.

I simply had to trust in that. Plus, the Sword was so close now. All I needed to do was figure out some way to pry it out of that damned wall.

Turning about, I marched through the gateway that led back to the temple, determined to do exactly that.

CHAPTER TWENTY-FIVE

With fast steps, I walked through the gateway and back into the temple. Glancing about, I noticed some things here have remained the same. Smaller arches still lined the walls. None of them were lit up, though. I cursed under my breath. Viktor promised to activate one of the gateways that would lead to Rowan. Not that seeing Rowan would help me right now, but the spell was supposed to be cast as a sign of good faith.

Viktor lied.

I scanned the chamber and gasped. There was no sign here of Nan, Mrefu, and Jicho. Viktor said that would be safe and protected. Rage tightened up my spine.

More lies.

Turning around, I inspected the large gateway behind me. This was the same archway I just passed through to meet Viktor. The light was gone and the gateway sealed shut.

If only that meant I had truly gotten rid of Viktor so easily.

No time to fret over my evil brother. I inspected the walls, searching for the Sword of Theodora. If I had enough hybrid magick to heal all the gateways, surely I could come up with some spell to pry one Sword off a wall.

But the Sword of Theodora was gone. An empty indentation sat in the wall now, the only sign that the blade had recently been there.

Damn.

Perhaps Nan, Jicho, and Mrefu had woken up and gotten the Sword free somehow. My Necromancer mind said that was the most logical explanation. I began the long trek back to the temple's entrance.

"Stop. You are forbidden to leave this temple," called a woman. I'd know that voice anywhere.

Amelia was here.

Spinning around, I saw dozens of figures step out from behind the many statues that lined the temple floor. More Caster warriors had arrived. Kade was here was well, and he carried a sleeping Jicho in his arms. Amelia now wore a long bronze cloak.

My breath caught. I'd seen that cloak before. All the statues in this room were a trio of figures. All of a sudden, I recognized them for what they were: a Not-Elea and Not-Viktor on their knees with a third figure standing behind them, holding the Sword of Theodora. It all added up to one horrible conclusion.

The descendant of Theodora was supposed to execute the Eleas and Viktors.

My dear friend Amelia was destined to kill me.

Even worse, my friend had a light blue glow under her skin. She was trapped in the power of a possession spell. I'd always felt some magick in the Sword hilt. It must be loaded with spells like any other totem. In my vision with Kila Kitu, the Sire and Lady has discussed loading some magick onto the blade. It seems they'd done just that.

And now, one of those spells was taking away Amelia's mind.

And this place? It could be nothing other than the Temple of Theodora. I lifted my hands, palms forward. "Don't do this, Amelia."

"Do what?" Amelia raised her arms. The Sword of Theodora was gripped in her fists. The light of possession danced across her skin.

I rounded on Kade. "Don't you see this? She's possessed!"

Kade glared in my direction. "She seems in her right mind to me." In other words, Kade wasn't going to stop this.

The glow on Amelia's skin was barely enough to register. If I hadn't been a trained Necromancer, I might not even have seen it. That means the spell was weakened, possibly because the Sword had been broken in half when the totem was created. I needed to get Amelia talking. Sometimes that broke people out of their possession. I gestured to the Sword. "How did you get that free?"

"It fell to the ground at my feet, because I am the rightful heir, not a fiend who kidnaps children and casts sleeping spells on them."

"They're still asleep? Viktor said he'd keep them safe. How can they be safe when they aren't even awake?"

"I knew it!" Kade roared. "What spell did you cast on Jicho and his friends? Take it away now."

"I had nothing to do with casting that spell. Believe me."

"Yet I don't believe you," said Amelia. "You're a kidnapper and liar. You deserve to die. The Sword of Theodora feels as good a way to kill you as any."

At those words, all the statues came to life again. The Eleas and Viktors raised their heads, opened their glassy eyes, and stared right at me. The executioners behind them lifted their arms. With a series of clicks, the metal hoods covering their faces fell away, revealing men and women who had a clear resemblance to Amelia. All were ready to wield their version of the Sword.

"Do you see this?" I pointed to the statues. "All these statues look like you. They were also placed under a spell by the magick of the sword. You're being manipulated into killing me and you don't even know why."

Amelia eyed the temple. For a moment, her features crumpled with confusion before firming up into a look of stony resolve.

"Grandfather told me the truth before he died. Justinian protected me from any knowledge of this temple for a reason. When the time comes, I would receive the Sword and know exactly how to use it. And that is precisely what is happening now. The Sword literally fell at my feet and here you are, casting evil spells on innocent children."

"I didn't do this. I can't cast any spells right now."

"That gateway wall is smashed," said Kade. "How did it get that way?"

"Yes, I can pull power into my body, but I can't recall how any incantations." I shook my head. "What I'm about to say may sound insane, but if you'll just let me hold the Sword for a moment, I swear, you'll remember exactly who I am and why we're really here. It's this spell from Mlinzi and Walinzi. It affects not only Rowan, but all the Casters except Jicho."

"You're right," said Amelia. "I don't believe you."

Amelia had been my friend through many adventures. Her mind was analytical and sharp. I needed to keep appealing to her logic.

"Will you answer me one question, Amelia?" She didn't reply, so I took that for agreement. "How did you know where to find me?"

Kade stepped forward. "That doesn't matter."

"No, I think it matters quite a lot. If I'm right, some Necromancer spell led you here. Perhaps you even knew it was cast by Viktor himself."

Amelia tilted her head. "What difference does that make?"

"Don't listen to her," warned Kade.

"Think, Amelia. You've the greatest mind I've ever known. If Viktor wants me dead or captured, doesn't that make me your ally? Isn't it worth a test just to let me hold the Sword for a moment?"

"And again, it all comes down to getting the damned Sword," said Kade. "Release my brother from your magick!"

"I told you. It's not my casting. It's Viktor's. You must recognize the spell signature, especially if you saw it in whatever casting led you to me."

Amelia eyed me up and down. I knew that look; she was considering my every word carefully. "You're a kidnapper and a thief. You deserve to die." Those statements came out more like questions, however. The light barely shone on her skin. I took that as progress.

"Shouldn't Rowan decide my fate?" I asked. "He is your king, after all. Only he can decide executions."

"Rowan isn't here," stated Kade. Even so, his words lacked the bite they had a moment ago. Kade could lose his temper when he felt his loved ones were threatened, but his anger was quick to cool. Hopefully, that was taking place right now.

"But one of these gateways could very well lead to Rowan. We can all approach him together."

Amelia smiled, but it was a look laced with despair. "I don't know…"

Kade moved to stand beside Amelia. "Maybe we should wait. She isn't attacking and it's against our code to kill in cold blood. Let's find Rowan. My brother will know how to help Jicho and his friends." Kade nodded to the warriors in the back of the chamber. They had strapped Nan and Mrefu onto stretchers.

"Yes, we should wait." Amelia tried to drop the Sword, but the item flashed with blue brightness, just like any other totem enacting a spell. Blue mist poured off the Sword, encasing Amelia in a sheen of azure brightness. Instead of dropping the weapon, Amelia raised the Sword high. Blue light poured from the blade. The weight of magick filled the air, enveloping me in its power.

I tried to move. I couldn't. Back in the Cloister, I'd read about layered magic totems like this one. If the right person touched the correct item, a spell became cast on both themselves and whoever they targeted. In this case, that would be Amelia and me. The only consolation in this spell was that although I couldn't move, I could still speak.

"This isn't right, Amelia. Don't you see that magick? It's making your decisions for you."

A magickal blue light now gleamed in Amelia's eyes. "I detect no spells."

"That's because the spell doesn't want you to." How many of Amelia's forebears had been compelled to kill? "You must stop this."

When Amelia spoke again, her voice was a low monotone. "No, you must give your magick back to the world. I will kill you and place your body on the gateway." The light from the blade glowed more brightly as she closed the space between us. My legs buckled on their own. Before I knew it, I was kneeling on the stone floor with my neck exposed, ready for her to strike. Cool waves of panic moved over my skin.

Amelia paused before me and raised the Sword high above her head. "This is for the good of all."

Suddenly, a voice rang through the temple. "Stop. She is not to be harmed *yet*." It was Rowan and his casting arm was bright with power as he spoke a quick incantation.

"End this."

The orb of red energy sped off his palm and into the Sword, landing onto the blade with a crackle of magick and light. The blue sheen of possession magick disappeared from Amelia's skin. I found that I, too, could move again.

Next Rowan himself stepped through the arch and into the temple. He seemed all things kingly and strong as he scanned the scene. After taking in his warriors, Jicho, Kade, and Amelia, Rowan's gaze landed on me.

"Everyone, follow me through the gateway." Rowan glared at me, hatred blazing in his green eyes. "I'll bring her."

I quickly considered my options. I still couldn't run from this temple—there were about twenty Caster warriors around, and I wasn't able to speak a single spell. But I had Rowan with me again, and we shared the power of mates. Maybe that would be enough to somehow set me loose, if only I could get him to willingly share power with me. Hybrid magick was also the best way to heal the gateways.

Rowan approached me, and I didn't even try to fight him. Leaning over, he quickly tied a rough cord around my wrists. I scanned his face, looking for any sign that he knew he was my mate. There was nothing; I still couldn't accept that.

"I'll convince you of who I am," I said in a low voice. "Believe me."

"Is that what you think?" Rowan shook his head. "That's impossible."

"Why? I still have a half day before the Martyr's Comet disappears, and the Sword is now in one piece. Where there is time, there is hope."

Rowan stepped back and eyed me carefully. He still kept a firm grip on the rope between us. "What are you playing at?"

"This is no game. I meant precisely what I said."

"You just spent six hours in that gateway with Viktor. The Martyr's Comet is about ready to vanish from the sky."

"Six hours?" Every muscle in my body seemed to stiffen. "That's not possible."

Rowan's full mouth thinned with a look of disgust. "What a sad lie. You're a Grand Mistress Necromancer. You know how mages can alter the perception of time. Didn't you sense any magick when you went to visit him?"

"Of course, but…"

Rowan folded his arms over his chest. "Please. Continue lying. I enjoy how you waste my time."

I knew my mate well enough to realize he could sense any untruth. I'd started to tell him something, and now I had to complete the thought. "I knew Viktor was casting a spell, but he'd told me that I was his sister. That news had me so overwhelmed, I didn't think through what he could be doing."

Rowan's stare turned intense. "You believe that, don't you?"

"I am his sister. The Sire and Lady are my parents. And you are my mate. That's all true."

A flicker of doubt shone in Rowan's green eyes, but it was gone too quickly to be certain. "Come along, crazy goddess." Rowan tugged on the ropes that held my hands secured. "It's time to meet your fate."

I followed him through the gateway, my heat pounding in my chest. One way or another, this would all be over soon.

CHAPTER TWENTY-SIX

I stepped out of the gateway and onto a familiar landscape. A long rectangular green stretched out before me, the grass colored in a checkerboard pattern of red and blue. Tall arches lined the space for as far as the eye could see, all of them glowing with a faint purple light.

The Meadow of Many Gateways.

Angling up my gaze, I scanned the skies, hoping that Rowan had somehow made an error. But there was no mistake. The Martyr's Comet hung low by the horizon line. It was almost ready to burst with light and power before it disappeared.

By any measure, I might only have a few minutes left to live.

I'd better make them count.

Suddenly, all the gateways glowed with pale purple light. Figures stepped out from the arches and onto the meadow. The Sire of Souls marched out first, followed by his massive army of knights in black armor. Next, the Lady of Creation emerged, along with her company of warriors in battle leathers. Each of her fighters was ethereally beautiful and accompanied by an animal familiar such as a massive lion, eagle, or serpent.

I fought back the urge to gasp. Such a formidable army, and they were all focused on one death. Mine.

Next, battalions of battle mages paraded out onto the field. My stomach lurched with recognition. All of these were Necromancers who had skull markings on their faces.

No question who their leader would be.

Sure enough, my one-time Mother Superior Petra strode in front of her Necromancer force. Since I'd last seen her, the lines in Petra's face had deepened, but the gleam in the elderly woman's eyes had only intensified. No doubt about it. Petra thought this was her great chance to serve the Sire and Lady. Her mind had been rotted out with ambition. She'd do nothing to help me.

Across the meadow, Rowan's Caster army strode through another gateway, taking their place beside the mortal Necromancer army. They all wore battle leathers and grim looks on their faces. I glanced over my shoulder at Rowan; he was eyeing his troops carefully.

"They look marvelous," I said in a low voice. "Kade has done well with them." About a month ago, Kade launched a new training program for their field fighters. The changes showed.

A muscle flicked by Rowan's jaw. "How would you know anything about that?"

"When Kade fell in love with my best friend, it changed him. He no longer thought it was glorious to lose your life in battle, especially when you consider the pain inflicted on the loved ones left behind. As a result, he's training them harder. You can even see it in the precision of their march. And the palace mages fight alongside them now as well. That's rather smart. I'm proud of Kade. This is sure to decrease casualties."

"Don't cast your—"

"I know, I know. I should keep my witchy powers to myself and not cast spells to see into your personal life."

"Right."

"I swear, you and your brothers have egos the size of Nyumbani. Do you really think the minutiae of Kade's love life is that interesting?"

For a moment, I saw the hint of a smile curl across Rowan's lips. It was gone too soon to be sure, though.

One last gateway was still spewing forth warriors. This time, it was Viktor who strode onto the field. Behind him, there came his army of Changed Ones. They were all in their mostly-human forms now, meaning they had only an arm or leg replaced with an animal part. That said, I had no doubt that Viktor would transform them into fully merged human-animal shapes when it suited him. A telltale glow emanated from all of their skin.

I pointed at the Changed Ones. This wasn't easy to do with my hands bound, but I managed. "Do you see the glow on those Changed Ones?"

"I do."

"Then do you know what it means?"

"Viktor is controlling them with a possession spell."

"The Changed Ones are still Casters. You can't let Viktor lead your people this way."

Rowan's gaze locked with mine. Hurt and hope swirled in his eyes, both in equal measure. "Why do you care?"

"You know why." I gestured again to the Changed Ones with my bound wrists. "I'm your mate and we need to free those Casters."

"What a courageous soul you have." Rowan ran his finger along my jawline. "Whoever you are, I'll miss you."

"I'm not going anywhere." This was pure bravado talking, but if I were about to die today, I might as well do it without cowering.

Across the meadow, the Lady and Sire stood side by side. They could be a painting, the two of them looked so perfect. The Lady stared at me and snapped her fingers. That part wasn't as lovely.

"I suppose that's her way of asking me over for a chat." In truth, I called to farm animals with more gentleness. "What a sweet mother I have."

"Shall we cross the meadow and speak with her?"

187

"Not yet." I dug in my heels and examined the Caster ranks. There were some faces missing. "Where are Nan, Mrefu, and Jicho?"

Rowan's eyes gentled. "They are with my army and still being transported on stretchers. Once this is all done, I'll cast healing spells to bring them back."

"Good. Thank you."

"You act so strangely for one of Viktor's kind."

"Because I'm not." My voice cracked with grief. "I keep telling you. I'm your mate. You have to know it's true."

For a moment, our gazes locked. The mate bond pulsed between us. A unique kind of energy filled the air. Somehow, I could sense Rowan's desire to kiss me once more.

I licked my lips slowly. "I want that as well, you know."

Rowan's brows drew together with confusion. "How could you know what I—"

The earth roiled beneath our feet. Great fissures opened in the checkerboard grasses. I'd seen all this before with Kila Kitu. The gateways were almost out of energy and our world would soon tear be torn apart. Every muscle in my body seemed to constrict with worry.

Across the meadow, the Lady raised her arms. It seemed that she'd given up on snapping and was moving up to larger gestures. "Come to us, dear daughter. Let us speak a while."

"Are those really your parents?" asked Rowan.

"It's true." My mind reeled with a thousand thoughts at once. I could try to escape, but that wasn't looking likely. I still couldn't cast a spell and Rowan, who could wield magick, didn't know who I was. The world was splitting apart and evidently, I might be the only person who could save it.

The Sire spoke next, his voice a deep rumble. "Come here, sweet daughter."

How many times had I craved to hear these words form my true parents? Only, I never imagined they would be spoken across a meadow lined with warriors who were ready to kill me. Life is strange when it gives you what you wish for.

I turned my attention to Rowan. "Let's go."

Without another word, Rowan and I began marching across the checkerboard ground. Our every footstep was in sync, as if our bodies remembered our mate connection, even if both our minds couldn't. As we closed in on the Lady and Sire, it took all my focus not to weep at their beauty. My mother was a vision with her sun-kissed skin, fair hair, and dancing green eyes. My father was all things austere, pale, and magnificent. The two of them looked so godlike, I could almost forget their betrayals.

Almost.

I paused before them. "Mother. Father."

"Dearest daughter," began the Lady. The lovely bell-like tones in her voice had me aching with sadness. How could someone who speaks so sweetly do such horrible things to her own blood? "Viktor told you who we really are."

"He did."

"I trust you're pleased," boomed the Sire.

"I'm not. All things being equal, I'd rather be back on Braddock Farm with Rosie."

"My child," said the Lady. "You must understand how horrible this is for us. If there were any way to save all this worlds from ruin without harming a hair on your head, then we would do it. But this is the only solution. And if you take the Sword willingly, it will be a much gentler passing."

Petra stepped forward from the crowd. "You're surrounded. It's hopeless. You must do what needs to be done. You should have taken on the Necromancer rule—and thereby accepted this fate—a long time ago. Your hesitance reflects poorly on all Necromancers."

I glared at Petra. "Ever since you figured out that I was the child of the gods, the only Necromancer you've cared about is yourself. You see me as your way into history. The Divine Petra, Mouthpiece of the Gods, Savior of the World, and whatever other nonsense titles you've dreamed up. Don't pretend this is about anything else but your own ambition. You're as greedy and selfish as my parents. I'm surprised your skin hasn't bubbled over like tar as well."

The Sire's eyes widened a fraction. It was the smallest movement, but still enough for me to notice. I switched my focus to him. "That's right. I know all about how you used hybrid magick to create these gateways. But then, you became drunk with power and the hybrid energy turned against you. Now you have to use this comet and your own children to maintain your empire. You disgust me."

Viktor stepped forward. This was a regular family reunion, if your family were made of corrupted gods and one adopted maternal figure who'd turned homicidal. "My cherished sister, you must listen to our parents. You were mishandled by Tristan and never taught how to properly live as a Necromancer." He turned to the Sire and Lady. "Kindest parents, you do her no favors by forestalling the inevitable. End this now."

"You're quite right, my son." The Lady waved toward the Caster army. "Bring forth the executioner."

Amelia stepped out from the line of warriors. She still wore the long bronze robes and grasped the Sword of Theodora in her fists. The hood was now pulled back, though, so I could see her large blue eyes and long red hair. Usually, her tresses were styled in neat ringlets. Now, they fell wildly over her shoulders. More blue light glowed on her skin, just as it did back in the Temple of Theodora. My heart sank. That brightness meant magick. Rowan hadn't defeated the totem spell on the Sword, only weakened it. I felt no need to kneel anymore, but Amelia was still under a compulsion spell to kill me.

Considering the ugly nature of this particular family reunion, it seemed fitting to add in a best friend who was also my executioner. Amelia marched stiffly across the green, pausing a few feet before me.

The moment didn't seem real. I was standing on a checkerboard meadow. My best friend wore bronze robes and wielded the Sword of Theodora. My parents and brother all watched on. My mate stood nearby, only he had absolutely no idea who I really was. With all my focus, I tried to picture some way out of this.

There was nothing.

The Sire pointed at me. "Kneel."

I didn't have any plan yet, but I knew I wasn't going to simply bow down to this death. "I refuse."

"Please kneel down, my daughter," said the Lady. "Trust us. Believe in our love for you. We wouldn't do this if there were any other way."

Her words echoed in my mind.

Trust.

Love.

My gaze locked on Rowan. Here stood my mate. If I believed in nothing else, I had to rely on the bond of love between us.

A plan appeared.

When I next spoke, I switched my focus between my parents. "I will do as you say, but I must die on my own terms. Rowan will wield the Sword."

"Let us consider this," said the Lady. My parents and Viktor then stepped aside to whisper quietly amongst themselves. All the while, my pulse beat with such force, I could feel its thud in my throat. The Lady's words kept ricocheting through my mind.

Love.

Trust.

My blood relations never truly understood these terms, or I wouldn't be standing here with a death sentence hanging over me. I had to rely on the fact that they couldn't imagine the true force of a mate bond. They had to agree to make Rowan my executioner.

Finally, the three of them ceased their whispering and returned to their place before the armies. My father was first to speak. "We agree to your terms," he said solemnly.

And with those five words, I had my first real hope that I might live.

The Lady gestured to Amelia. "Give this Caster mortal your Sword, child of the House of Theodora."

With wooden movements, Amelia lurched over to Rowan and handed him the Sword. My mate gripped the hilt and turned to face me. If he felt any hesitation to murder me, Rowan didn't show it in his face.

"Caster mortal," said the Sire. "Our daughter has requested that you kill her. This is a great honor. Since Elea does this willingly, all you need do is touch the Sword to her skin anywhere. She will pass on peacefully."

"That's right." Raising my bound arms, I turned my palms toward Rowan. This was a motion I'd done many times before as I'd begged Rowan to share hybrid power. "All I need is a touch."

Rowan stalked closer, lifting the Sword high above his head. I kept my gaze locked with his and my arms outstretched. If my mate was going to kill me, let it be this way.

Rowan paused before me. One emotion after another washed over his face. Rage. Confusion. Love.

Which one would win out?

With a great swoop, Rowan brought the Sword down. I held my breath, my body tensing for the blow. It never came. At the last second, Rowan dropped the Sword and gripped my hands in his. Instantly, I felt his energy and magick pour though our connected palms.

"We are mates," whispered Rowan. "My heart knew it all along."

With those words, everything started happening at once. Viktor, Petra, and my parents all called for their armies to attack. I leaned over, desperate to grab the Sword of Theodora, regain my knowledge of how to cast, and restore Rowan's full memories.

A thousand voices rang out in battle calls.

The ground rumbled with countless footfalls.

The skies darkened with flying birds of prey, all of them mounted with more fighters.

My fingertips brushed the Sword's hilt and then, it happened.

The totem ring on my finger lit up with orange light. This was the band that had been given to me by Mlinzi and Walinzi, three days and a hundred years ago. I had just enough time to look over to Rowan. Mlinzi and Walinzi had transformed his mating band into an orange totem ring as well. And it was also lighting up with magick.

A haze of orange fog instantly surrounded us both. My body felt torn in a thousand directions at once as the totem rings launched their spells and transported me and Rowan away. Even so, I stayed focused on one thing.

The Sword of Theodora was in my grasp at last.

I wasn't letting go.

CHAPTER TWENTY-SEVEN

The next thing I knew, I stood in an orange jungle. A tangerine sun blazed down upon me. Humidity pressed in all around. I'd returned to the land of Mlinzi and Walinzi. Even better, my mate was here as well.

I gripped the Sword tightly against my chest. It wasn't an easy movement, considering how my hands were still bound. "Rowan?" It was an effort to force out every word. "Do you remember me?"

The strong lines of his face melted into a massive smile. "Elea." He gripped the cords around my wrists, tearing the heavy ropes apart like they were paper.

My heart soared with joy. My Rowan was back.

Tossing the Sword aside, I leapt up and wrapped my arms around Rowan's neck. He gripped my waist, pulling me against him. We shared a feverish kiss that somehow gathered together everything beautiful in my life. Passion. Joy. Trust.

Lowering my arms, I laced my fingers with my mate's. My soul craved us to share power. It was the most natural process in the world to pull fresh Necromancer energy into my body and then press it to Rowan's. We quickly formed a loop of magick, the power swirling though both of us, brightening our skin with purple light as our mouths tangled in a deepening kiss. It was a perfect moment and I wanted it to last forever.

The ground shook once, then twice, as a pair of massive somethings landed nearby. Rowan and I broke our kiss to find Mlinzi and Walinzi towering over us. They were just as I remembered them: massive, tall, and orange.

"He looks delicious," growled Mlinzi. "Can we have him for dinner?"

Walinzi swatted her brother on the shoulder, a movement that caused the nearby jungle trees to bend into the resulting wind. "Quiet now," scolded Walinzi. "We're about to be free from the threat of those two itsy bitsy tyrants." She leaned down until her nose holes were inches from my face. "You have the Sword and your mate, along with some new knowledge. Tell me. Don't you think your parents deserve death?"

I bit back a groan. In all the commotion, I'd forgotten how Mlinzi and Walinzi wanted me to murder the Sire and Lady. I turned to Rowan. "Meet Mlinzi and Walinzi. They're rather intent on killing the Sire and Lady."

Rowan wrapped his arm around my shoulder. "I know who they are. Now, I can remember everything that happened after these two took my memories. As for the request to kill, I don't think we should do anything they wish, let alone commit murder."

"Come now, little one." Walinzi leaned back on her haunches. "We're tricksters. We wanted to help you, but we had to do it in our own way."

"Now you kill for us," cried Mlinzi. "Kill!"

"You're in no position to demand anything," I said. "You still haven't kept to your side of the bargain. Back at the Meadow of Many Gateways, the Martyr's Comet is about to disappear."

Walinzi pretended to be very interested in grooming her fur. "What of it?"

"My world is about to be destroyed. You promised me two things: the Sword of Theodora and the knowledge of how to heal the gateways."

Mlinzi grinned, showing an impossible number of blade-like teeth. "You want to know how to cast spells with hybrid magick."

"That's right," I said. "That was our agreement."

After scooping up the Sword from the jungle floor, Rowan pulled me against him once more. I knew my mate. He was prepared to fight for this information, if needed.

Walinzi rocked on her haunches and laughed. The sound was so loud, a flock of tangerine-colored birds flew out from nearby trees. "She wants to know how to cast hybrid spells! Cast!"

Mlinzi hopped up and down, making the ground shake further. "She wants incantations! Ha!"

"What do you..." The words stopped in my throat as my mind reeled through everything I knew about hybrid magick. I'd noticed how Kila Kitu never used incantations to cast a spell. And based on how hybrid magick corrupted, everything about it seemed to work on intent. I focused on Rowan. "When you cast those cords with hybrid magick, how did that happen?"

"You mean back at the Skullock Passage?"

"Yes, when you saved me."

Rowan's eyes glazed over as he searched through his own memories. "I simply thought how much I wanted to save you."

"That's it. Hybrid magick works based on will. It's an energy all to itself—its own life force"

Rowan nodded slowly. "So the magick decides how to execute the mage's commands."

"Yes, and when the power is corrupted, it can only cause damage. That's why the Sire and Lady can't heal the gateways on their own. Their hybrid magick has turned against them. It's the same thing that happened to Viktor. His power soured as well."

"So we can go back and simply ask the magick to heal the gateways."

"I think so."

Rowan beamed. "Let's make the journey."

"Not so quickly," said Walinzi. "We can't leave before we know your full plans."

"Kill!" Mlinzi cried. "Kill! Kill!"

"We got that part, dear." Walinzi waved off her brother. "You two mortals aren't leaving our realm until I have your word that you'll murder the Sire and Lady."

"No," I said.

"Maim them?" asked Walinzi.

"No." This was getting repetitive.

"Maybe frighten them a little, then."

"Our previous agreement still stands," I said. "You will not be subject to their rule."

"No kill?" asked Mlinzi. We all ignored him.

Walinzi lowered her voice to a whisper, which coming from her massive form was no whisper at all. "Fine. Kill them or don't, I'm not a particular monkey. Just set us free from the threat of those two puny terrors or we'll destroy you both slowly. Understood?"

"We understand," I said. I still didn't know exactly how I would free the tricksters' realm, but Rowan and I had a few minutes to scheme. We'd figure something out. Hopefully.

"Good," said Walinzi. "Now, off with you. Back to the meadow."

With that, the totem rings on our fingers flared once more with orange light. Rowan and I became encased in a haze of power as we were wrenched back to the Meadow of Many Gateways...And without any time to come up with a real plan.

Mlinzi and Walinzi had tricked us again.

CHAPTER TWENTY-EIGHT

A moment later, the transport spell ended. Once again, Rowan and I stood on the Meadow of Many Gateways. The Martyr's Comet flared with crimson light, casting everything in a blood red glow. Five armies still waited on the checkerboard ground, ready to attack. I counted the warriors of the Lady, Sire, Viktor, Petra, and Rowan. Thousands of eyes were now locked on Rowan and me. Waiting.

The Lady broke the silence. "You've come back to us. Are you ready for your sacrifice?"

I turned to Rowan and lifted my arm, palm forward. The request was there but unspoken. *Let's share hybrid power so we can attack.*

Rowan curved his full mouth into the hint of a smile. "My brave mate. It will take some time to pull in enough magick." Which made sense. We'd never attempted anything so huge with hybrid power before, and it took time to pull in our energy and transform it.

"In that case, we better get started."

Rowan rested his palm against mine. Both of us pulled in our respective magick. Then the power moved between us, sending beams of violet light up our arms and across our chests, spinning through each other in great loops. Rowan still held the Sword of Theodora in his right hand. He raised it high until the light of the Martyr's Comet reflected off the blade.

At that sight, all the Casters broke out into a massive cheer. Evidently, they'd all regained their memories and knew precisely who I was. They seemed beyond thrilled that Rowan and I now had the Sword. I wouldn't be surprised if they left the field of battle to start yet another celebration.

For their part, the Sire and Lady frowned. Viktor's face flushed with rage. The Sire stepped forward, his face tight with anger. "You see the armies arrayed before you, daughter. You are our flesh and blood, and we don't want to send our forces to attack you, but we will."

The Lady glanced over toward Petra. "Or perhaps some mortals will do so for us."

My mouth fell open with shock. My parents never liked killing their children themselves, but they weren't above ordering someone else to do their dirty work.

Across the meadow, Petra understood exactly what the deities wanted. She began shrieking at the Necromancers. "Attack Elea! Save yourselves!"

One of the Necromancers stepped forward. I recognized him as Quinn, someone I'd raised from the dead after the battle with Viktor. He was a tall man with skull-like features, even before he'd received the bone markings on his face. "Our Tsarina is trying to save us. Don't you see?"

Petra rounded on him. "She's supposed to sacrifice herself, not cast a hybrid spell or whatever it is she's doing. Her death is what the Sire and Lady want. We can be part of that history."

"I won't hurt her." Quinn gestured behind him. "Neither will the others. Our Tsarina raised us all from the dead."

I could have shouted for joy. Despite Petra's urgings, the Necromancer army stayed in place. This gave me and Rowan critical time to pull in more power. Hybrid energy zinged through my limbs, but there was still more room in my soul for magick. Rowan and I would need every last bit we could gather.

Petra turned to Rowan's Casters, who still stood beside her on the meadow. "This witch has entranced you! Don't you want her gone?"

Kade stepped forward. "Didn't you hear our cries of joy? We'll protect our king and his mate until the end."

Amelia stood at Kade's side, her face streaked with tears. She called to me across the meadow. "Kade told me what happened. I didn't know what I was doing, Elea." Her bronze robes were torn at the neckline. "We'll fight for you now. I swear!"

Rowan shook his head. "Stay where you are, all of you. Elea and I will end this. No bloodshed."

The Lady grinned. "I knew you didn't want a fight. You're summoning hybrid power for another reason.."

"They're trying to heal the gateways for us," said the Sire. "But that's not how we want it done. You'd be too dangerous afterwards. Hybrid power always corrupts."

In other words, they fear having a couple around who was stronger than they were. More hybrid energy built up in every corner of my being. My parents would have to learn to live with disappointment. Soon, there would be a stronger pair of mages in this world.

"Please, just sacrifice yourself willingly." The Lady raised her arm, and the Sword of Theodora flew into her palm. "Allow me to ease your passing. I'll deliver the blow myself, that's a great honor for you."

"We're not going to heal the gateways," I said.

"Good." The Sire's face turned into a mask of calm once more. "Go to your mother now."

"We're going to blow them apart, just like we did to the Skullock Passage."

"What?" The Sire's normally calm face twitched with rage. "You can't mean that. This empire is ours."

"Your empire is over," I said. "Welcome to the end of the Meadow of Many Gateways."

Viktor waved to me from the spot with his army. "So you're gifting me this realm? Thank you."

I knew what my brother meant. By closing the gateways, I'd lock my parents here, right where he could kill them. After that, Viktor would rule this world.

But I didn't have time right now to worry about Viktor and his scheming. My parents had rallied together. Standing side by side, they called out the same word in unison.

"Attack!"

The armies of black knights and leather clad warriors raced toward us. The ground rumbled with their footfalls. One again, the skies darkened with airborne fighters. I turned to Rowan. An eerie sense of calm washed over me. My body felt so crammed with power, it seemed ready to burst.

"Are you ready, my mate?" I asked.

Rowan nodded. "Let's send these armies back to the Eternal Lands."

We didn't need to speak an incantation. Our intention was enough for the hybrid magick. All of a sudden, purple cords wound down our arms. The ropes gleamed with magick and power, and they wanted to be set loose. Like the pull of a magnet, the ethereal ropes summoned us to stop pressing our palms together and instead face out toward the oncoming army.

We weren't so much casting a spell as having a conversation with magick.

Rowan and I both turned to face the oncoming forces.

The cords of light and power burst forth from our arms, multiplying as they shot out across the open meadow. From the corner of my eye, I saw Petra screaming at my Necromancers, urging them to join the battle. None of my people moved into the fray.

My people? Since when did I think of them as this?

The answer appeared in a flash. The Necromancers became mine once they decided to fight for me. I would never back down from an ally. After all, I was casting this hybrid spell to keep faith with a pair of tricksters. I could do no less than for my fellow mages.

The magickal ropes tied themselves around every warrior. Cords wound around waists of fighters. More entangled about the legs of horses. Thousands shot into the sky, tying up the wings of flying creatures. Others bound the hands and feet of the Sire and Lady.

Meanwhile, the palace mages had cast spells to contain the Changed Ones. Kade wasn't standing around idle; he'd ordered the Caster mages to help. Now, all the Changed ones were restrained in a great Orb of Holding. It essentially looked like a great glass container that kept them all in place.

Good work, Kade.

Without words, the hybrid magick told me that it had everyone from the Eternal Lands in its grasp. I turned to Rowan. "Do you sense it?" I didn't need to say that it was the fact that the magick was ready to send everyone back. Rowan could hopefully sense it as well as I did.

Rowan nodded. "It's time they went home."

After that, the magick knew exactly what Rowan and I wanted. Instantly, the violet cords snapped loose from our arms. After that, the free ends sped into different gateways, lighting them up with violet brightness. Moving in sync, the magickal ropes yanked the warriors through the arches. As each fighter passed on, the gateways flared with purple light.

My heart soared. The hybrid magick was working. Soon, the only people left on the meadow would be the Caster and Necromancer armies. The Changed Ones were still secure inside the Orb of Holding. Petra kept screaming at my people, but they weren't heeding her, despite the fact that her arm blazed with Necromancer power, ready to cast a spell. That didn't bode well.

I focused on my hybrid magick. "Go after Petra." The cords of power didn't respond.

Rowan added his voice into the mix. "Get rid of that Mother Superior."

Closing my eyes, I connected with the new energy inside my soul. Rowan and I had pulled in a lot of power, but I could tell that the hybrid energy had enough to do with dragging off the Sire of Souls, Lady of Creation and all their minions. Petra would simply have to wait.

I looked to Rowan. "The magick needs more time."

"I sense it as well. Once the hybrid power is done with the residents of the Eternal Lands, it will focus on the rest." His emerald gaze held mine, and all things confident shown in his eyes. "We can do this."

"What about Viktor? I haven't seen the cords grab him. The magick might see him as a resident of our world, not the Eternal Lands." There was also the fact that our world was about to implode and there were gateways to heal, but I figured we needed to pace out our worries.

"Good point," said Rowan. "I'll keep an eye out for Viktor. You watch Petra."

"Agreed."

There was no sign of Viktor, but Petra was easy enough to find. Her arm still glowed blue with power as she berated my Necromancers. The sight made blood boil. That is, until another scene grabbed my attention entirely.

My parents were being pulled through the gateways. All the other residents of the Eternal Lands had already vanished, but the Sire and Lady remained and fought against their bonds, twisting, writhing and fighting every step of the way. The cords stayed wrapped about their hands and waists, but the two dug their heels into the meadow. Hauling them into the gateways was slow going.

"Do you see that?" I asked Rowan.

"Hard to miss."

"We need to send in more power."

"Right."

Focusing deep within our souls, Rowan and I delved into every corner of our consciousness, heaving forth every last scrap of hybrid power we could manage. Before, my body had felt so jammed with hybrid magick, I thought I might explode. Now, my limbs felt empty and hollow. Even when my blood had been drained by Kila Kitu, I hadn't felt this woozy.

Our efforts soon paid off. The violet cords around the Sire and Lady turned thicker and stronger. Suddenly, the ropes flared more brightly than ever before. The cords turned taught and whipped my parents out of this world and through a gateway. Light flared as they disappeared.

Seeing that, something in my soul broke. I'd wanted to know my parents so badly, thinking there was a hole in my heart without them. Now, I realized how much I already had. Rowan, Amelia, Jicho, Rosie…I'd had a loving and full life indeed. My parents were better off where they were, in their own realm while I stayed in mine.

For a moment, the meadow was silent. The Caster and Necromancer armies looked to us expectantly. The Changed Ones were still sealed inside their Orb of Holding. Above us, the red light of the Martyr's Comet burned more intensely than ever.

That's when Viktor struck.

My brother had hidden himself inside the Necromancer army. It was easy enough to do, considering how he was already wearing hooded Necromancer robes.

Now, Viktor leapt out from the ranks of death mages. In all the excitement of dispelling the other armies, somehow the Lady had dropped the Sword of Theodora. Or perhaps she gave it to her son. In any case, Viktor now held the Sword in his fist.

And he was racing toward Rowan and me.

The Necromancer and Caster armies roared with rage. That's when Petra got into the battle as well. She released the magick she'd been storing up and quickly cast a skeletal wall. This was a massive structure made of thousands of razor-sharp bones, and it blocked the Caster and Necromancer armies. The Changed Ones were left outside the wall, however. I assessed the Orb of Holding that kept them back. The Changed Ones were pounding against the pearlescent walls. Cracks had already formed in the sphere. It wouldn't last much longer.

Kade could order the palace mages to cast a few spells and shore up the Orb of Holding, but all of Rowan's people were still blocked behind Petra's Bone Wall, along with Petra herself. Rowan and I could boost up the Orb of Holding as well, but we'd both depleted our magick in order to get rid of the Sire and Lady. And I couldn't speak for Rowan, but I not only felt empty, I was exhausted too. My mind felt numb from processing so much magick. Normally, I'd rest for days after what I'd just done. Here, there was no time.

Viktor raised his fist, showing off the totem rings that gleamed on his fingers. He called out the words to launch the spells hidden within the bands. "Attack!" Blue lights flared as the hidden spells came to life.

This was where all Viktor's planning came into play. His totem spells were all about empowering his army of Changed Ones. Before, the Changed Ones had been mostly human. Now, they all transformed into full hybrids of humans and animals. Lions, eagles, and reptiles…every kind of predator now stood across the meadow from us. They beat against the wall of the Orb of Holding with ferocious power.

The spell burst apart. The Changed Ones were free.

Viktor raced toward us with a hoard of berserk animal warriors behind him. The Sword of Theodora gleamed in his fist.

I searched my soul, looking for any kind of hybrid power left inside me. I was empty. My gaze locked with Rowan's. "I've no magick left. You?"

Rowan shook his head and raised his hand. "We need to recharge."

I pressed my palm against his and tried to pull Necromancer power into my body. Exhaustion was getting the better of me. No matter how hard I pushed myself, I could only pull in a thin trickle of blue light. Pathetic.

Rowan wasn't doing much better himself. "I'm too tired. I can't recharge."

"We need help." My gaze ran across the orange totem ring on my own hand. An idea formed. "Whatever power you have, focus it into your totem ring. Maybe we can summon Mlinzi and Walinzi." It was an outlandish plan, but as least it was one.

"Right." Rowan glared at his own totem ring with such intensity, I was surprised the metal didn't disintegrate under his stare.

For my part, I channeled my paltry bit of Necromancer energy into my orange band while repeating the same thoughts, over and over. *"We need you. Help us."*

At the same time, Viktor and his army of Changed Ones rampaged closer. Viktor ran before his warriors, a maniacal gleam in his eyes.

I stared down at my hand. The last time the totem ring activated, it glowed orange. Now, the metal looked ordinary and dull. The same was true with Rowan's ring.

The plan to summon the trickster gods wasn't working.

Time to fight.

It took a huge effort, but I was able to force myself to face turn and face Viktor straight on. I imagined myself standing strong and tall but in reality, I mostly wobbled. Reaching out with my mage senses, I pulled in whatever Necromancer energy I could find. Another pathetic stream of power wound up my arm. If I got lucky, I might be able to cast a fireball spell. One.

Rowan stood by my side. His hand glowed red, too, and the light of his magick was just as weak as mine.

Viktor was closing in.

Twenty yards.

Ten.

One.

My brother paused before us and raised the Sword of Theodora high. "I told you that you'd power the gateways for me. Thank you for my empire."

He never got the chance to lower his blade.

All of a sudden, the gateway behind us flared with orange light. The stone arch burst as two gigantic monkeys leapt onto the meadow. It was Mlinzi and Walinzi, and they were angrier than I'd ever seen them.

"Kill!" cried Mlinzi.

Viktor stood frozen in shock, the blade still held above in head. "What in the worlds are you?"

Walinzi pursed her long lips. "I've seen this one. He causes you trouble, doesn't he, Elea?"

"He was about to run me through with a sword, actually." I was proud of how little I slurred my words.

"Yes, brother. You may kill him. Use the Sword."

Mlinzi hopped up and down, crying out "ooo-ooo-ooo" noises as he swiped the Sword of Theodora from Viktor and jammed the blade through my brother's chest. A beam of crimson light flared up from the wound. At the same time, the last rays of the Martyr's Comet cast the meadow in a blood-red glow.

Viktor howled, pain etched into his pale features. He wasn't a willing sacrifice, and agony was the result. It felt as if a year slowly passed while he died. In reality, it was probably a matter of seconds before my brother was gone.

The meadow's grounds rumbled beneath our feet. Great fissures opened up in the earth. The Martyr's Comet flared its brightest shade of red yet. We were almost out of time.

"Quickly," I said. "We need to place Viktor's body on the gateway."

Rowan bent down to lift Viktor in his arms, but Walinzi was too fast for him. She scooped up my brother's body and chucked it into a nearby gateway with all the ceremony of tossing out an old banana peel. I suppose that's what she thought of him in the end: garbage.

Like I'd seen in the vision with Kila Kitu, Viktor's dead body flared with violet light, a brightness that seeped into the gateway around him before being transferred into the surrounding arches. One by one, the nearby gateways lit up with searing violet light. The earth rumbled as the great breaks in the ground pressed back together.

Our world was healing.

Viktor was dead.

It didn't seem possible, but it was happening all the same. I made a mental note to visit every Seer and spell Caster who'd said it was impossible for Viktor to become the sacrifice and explain to them what had actually happened. In detail.

The light from the Martyr's Comet disappeared. Viktor's body became transparent as a ghost's, and then he was gone as well.

Across the meadow, the Bone Wall cast by Petra crumbled into dust. Beyond it, I could see how the Necromancers and Casters had turned into a combined army in order to defeat Petra. Her body lay lifeless on the earth. My eyes stung with sadness. She hadn't been evil so much as weak, and it cost her everything.

Walinzi plunked down beside me, fanning herself with the end of her long orange tail. "You've locked the Sire and Lady back in their home realm. It seems you and your mate are now rulers of an empire. What do you plan to do with it?"

There was no question on that count. I turned to Rowan. "Are you thinking the same that I am?"

Rowan gave me one of his most crooked smiles. "We'll hold a festival that will be the greatest ever seen."

"Precisely. We'll need to be crowned—both of us—and we'll hold the ceremony right here. You and Mlinzi are invited, of course."

Walinzi kept fanning herself with her tail. "We'll check our schedule."

Across the meadow, the Caster army whooped with joy. Many pulled out skins of whiskey and passed them around. Another group broke into song, the words lauding all the glories of Rowan and me. A few Necromancers even joined in the tune.

And right here, in this moment, the world was perfect.

CHAPTER TWENTY-NINE

Rowan and I stood at the far end of the Meadow of Many Gateways. Casters and Necromancers alike milled around the periphery of the long rectangular grounds, waiting for the festival to start.

Technically, they had to get through our coronations before the festival actually began, but that was a minor point in Caster culture. My Necromancers joined in the fun, not drinking themselves silly, but not sitting in a corner speaking in monotones, either. Also within the crowds roamed many Changed Ones. With Viktor dead, they were no longer a threat and could be reunited with their families. It had been sad work, but our palace mages had found the dead bodies of the Changed Ones that Viktor had killed in testing out his army. Over the past weeks, we'd held mourning ceremonies for all those lost. It had been a hard month for my Caster people.

But that was over now and a coronation was about to begin. I wore my formal Caster gown, which was little more than a band of leather that covered my chest, hips and waist. I'd paired it with a hooded black cloak to celebrate my Necromancer rule as well. Rowan had done the same. He wore his leather trousers and nothing to cover his chest, paired with another black cloak to match mine. We were going to become Genesis Rex and Regina, Tsarina and Tsar.

Or we would do so once our guests of honor arrived: Mlinzi and Walinzi were expected at any moment.

In the meantime, everyone else seemed to already be here. Kade, Amelia, and Jicho were in the crowd, along with Nan, Mrefu, and a good number of the Zaidi. Even Amelia's brother Philippe and his new wife had journeyed in for the occasion. Philippe was now married to none other than Veronique, another woman with Necromancer power who'd been imprisoned with me in the Midnight Cloister. I could never imagine that girl being happy, but Veronique positively beamed with joy as she walked about at Philippe's side. Another young survivor from the Midnight Cloister, the six-year-old Ada, trailed along with them as well. Ada was now their adopted daughter. Somewhere during the last few months, Philippe and Veronique had resolved their differences, eloped, and adopted a child. One of these days, I'd have to corner them and get the full tale.

Behind us, a gateway flared with orange light as Mlinzi and Walinzi burst onto the scene. As always, the ground shook as they landed beside us.

"You're late," I said to Walinzi.

She gave me a sly grin. "Just because we've decided to permanently live in your world, it doesn't make you the rulers of me and my brother. We answer to no one."

"Kill," said Mlinzi. These days, that was his stock answer to everything. Walinzi said it was nothing to worry over, so I tried to ignore it.

Rowan turned to me. "Are you ready to start us off?"

"Mostly." I'd been successfully avoiding public speaking. Now that I was ascending my thrones, that time was over.

"You'll dazzle them, I know it."

Rowan raised his arms and the meadow fell quiet. Every set of eyes seemed trained on me. He lowered his arms again; this was my signal to start.

I cleared my throat. Now, I could use magick to enhance the sound of my voice, but Rowan and I planned a major casting for today, and I needed all my power for that spell. Instead, I simply spoke as loudly as I could. "My people, Necromancers and Casters! Today, Rowan and I stand before you as your Genesis Rex and Regina, your Tsarina and Tsar. Normally, this coronation would involve hours of ceremony, rites, and speeches, but I know my Caster subjects wouldn't appreciate that." Some of the Caster folks cheered at this.

As we'd planned, Rowan then continued the speech. "However, this morning is about a new era and doing things differently. Elea and I wield new hybrid powers now, and that means change. The old ways must be ended. Never again will someone need to sacrifice themselves with the Martyr's Comet. Elea and I have another way to keep our world safe."

It was my turn to speak again. "Plus, we know how our people enjoy a nice display of magick." The Casters cheered once more. I was fairly certain some of them had already started celebrating, even though it was fairly early in the morning. "So without further ado, we invite you to witness the launch of our new regime." I looked over to Rowan. "Ready?"

"Absolutely." In this moment, all the love in the world seemed to shine in his eye. I couldn't imagine a better way to start our new ceremony and life together.

Moving in unison, Rowan and I knelt down and set our palms flush against the ground. We'd spent days sharing energy and hybrid power. Now, both of us were ready to cast the mother of all spells. As we'd learned, all we had to do was ask our hybrid power for help.

"We're ready to begin," I said.

"Free these worlds," added Rowan.

Instantly, cords of violet power wound down our arms and burrowed their way into the earth. The hybrid magick had begun its work. Seconds later, purple ropes of light and power burst up again from the ground, winding themselves around the gateways closest to Rowan and me. After that, the cords moved on to the next archways, and the next. Soon, every arch on the Meadow of Many Gateways was buried under tangled layers of light, ropes, and magick. It was a beautiful sight.

Closing my eyes, I gave the hybrid power one final command. "Now."

A series of deafening booms sounded as one after the other, the gateways burst into rubble, closing off any access to the other realms and leaving us safely in our own. The crowd toasted, cheered, and sang. Some children began crawling up the tails of Walinzi and Mlinzi, who then proceeded to give monkey-back rides to anyone who asked, so long as they were children. The adults were invited on their backs only to be summarily dumped off again by "accident." These were trickster gods, after all. No one truly expected them to change.

And so, the festival of our coronation had begun.

Now that the gateways were gone, I stood once more, as did Rowan. I looped my arms about his waist and leaned into his chest, simply because I could.

"You know something?" I asked.

"Tell me."

"This may actually be the greatest festival of all time."

"Indeed." Rowan gave me one of his most beautiful grins, the one where his dimples popped out. "Well, now that you're queen, you need to join in the fun. Are you ready, my mate?"

And in that moment I did feel ready, but in more ways than one. Sure, I was about to join a party. More importantly, I was truly ready to embrace a future with my mate. And like our bond, I trusted in that completely.

The End

ACKNOWLEDGEMENTS

It's so awesome to finally share this book with you! Honestly, I've been DYING to blab about the dozen or so reveals in this final installment. I hope you enjoyed reading them, because it's been a serious strain on my limited ability to keep secrets. I can't even hide holiday gifts from my husband for more than six hours, tops. And I've been waiting on this book for years!

Well, that's enough about the book and all its reveals. Let's move onto the totally awesome people who made it possible. To begin with, I would like to send a massive thank-you out to my readers. I have a lot of cool fans, but the ones who love Beholder? You are the best and truest lovers of unique fantasy in the universe, end of story. I absolutely adore how excited you get for this series, and your enthusiasm kept me going through long nights and extra revisions. You are amazing.

Next, I must bow down to the incredible folks at INscribe Digital, who move mountains and make it look easy. This includes the wonderful Kelly Peterson, Kimberly Lane, Katy Beehler, Alli Davis, Ana Szaky, and Larry Norton. You all are totes awesome.

Also, a big welcome to the new team at IPG; I look forward to getting to know you all!

Behind the scenes is a team of crazies who keep me writing and happy. Top of the list is my kick-ass editor, Genevieve Iseult Eldredge. It's been a joy to work with you, and I can't wait to see what the future holds. And Arely Zimmermann? I'd be a mess without you. M-E-S-S. No lie.

Best for last. Huge and heartfelt thanks to my husband and son. None of this would be possible without my guys. First and last, you two are my everything.

Also from Christina Bauer:
The Paranormal Romance Best Seller, *Angelbound*

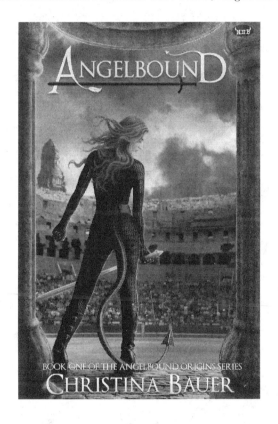

Also From Christina Bauer:
A New Shifter Romance, The Fairy Tales of the
Magicorum Series

Also From Christina Bauer:
The Snarky Dystopian Series, *Dimension Drift*

Also From Monster House Books,
The Urban Fantasy Romance Series, *Circuit Fae*

Christina Bauer thinks that fantasy books are like bacon: they just make life better. All of which is why she writes romance novels that feature demons, dragons, wizards, witches, elves, elementals, and a bunch of random stuff that she brainstorms while riding the Boston T. Oh, and she includes lots of humor and kick-ass chicks, too. Christina lives in Newton, MA with her husband, son, and semi-insane golden retriever, Ruby.

Don't miss out on the latest discounts, news and release updates from Christina Bauer and Monster House Books!

Sign up for our newsletter

http://tinyurl.com/iwantMHB